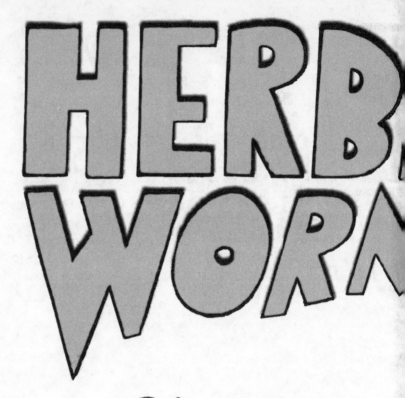

Peter Nelson

ERT'S
MHOLE

Rohitash Rao

HARPER
AN IMPRINT OF HARPERCOLLINS*PUBLISHERS*

Herbert's Wormhole

Library of Congress Cataloging-in-Publication Data

Nelson, Peter.

Herbert's wormhole / Peter Nelson & Rohitash Rao. — 1st ed.

p. cm.

Summary: When almost-sixth-grader Alex, a video game fanatic, is
forced on a playdate with his neighbor Herbert, an inventor, the two
travel to the twenty-second century and face off against aliens, who are
not as beneficent as most people think.

ISBN 978-0-06-168868-3 (trade bdg.)

[1. Time travel—Fiction. 2. Extraterrestrial beings—Fiction.
3. Inventors—Fiction. 4. Video games—Fiction.] I. Rao, Rohitash.
II. Title.

PZ7.N43583Her 2009   2008035299

[Fic]—dc22   CIP

                                                          AC

Typography by Alison Klapthor

09 10 11 12 13 LP/RRDB 10 9 8 7 6 5 4 3

❖

First Edition

To Charlie, and all the times you asked to hear
just one more bedtime story. —P.N.

For you, Mom.

Sorry chemistry didn't work out. —R.R.

ACKNOWLEDGMENTS

We'd like to thank from the bottom of our hearts Richard Winkler, Tina Wexler, Jordan Brown, Karina Kliss, Alison Klapthor, David Caplan, and Dominie Mahl for all they did to help us bring our story to life.

And the Nelson and Rao families, whose ever-present love, patience, support, and inspiration allow us the faith and freedom to create stories like this.

And finally to our own personal alien slayer, Brenda Bowen, who has a gazillion more stories just waiting for the great fortune to meet her in the future.

—Pete and Ro

CHAPTER

Alex Filby aimed his blaster at the very last Alien Invader, then hesitated before pulling the trigger.

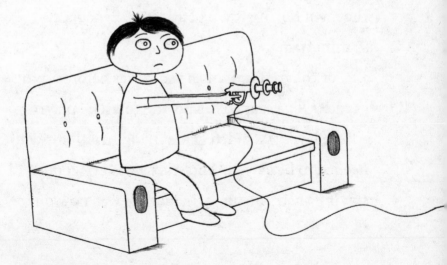

His mom smiled. "Your father's right, Sweetie. *Laser-fry that space-bug's scaly butt!*"

Alex sighed and looked out his bedroom window. Merwinsville, he thought, had to be the most boring town of all time. Especially summertime.

For the first half of the summer before sixth grade, Alex escaped his boring town by playing AlienSlayer 2, a video game involving aliens who needed to be slayed. And Alex was very good at slaying them. So good, in fact, he was now one trigger-squeeze away from slaying the very last Alien Invader, saving planet Earth, and reaching the end of the game. But instead of being excited,

he was hesitant. Worried, even.

Right when vacation started, Alex had begged his mom and dad for AlienSlayer 2. He promised them that as soon as he completed it, he'd put it away, play outside, and not ask for another video game for the rest of the summer.

Big mistake.

The day after he'd made that stupid promise, AlienSlayer:3-D!, the greatest video game in the history of video games, arrived in stores. AS:3-D!

had motion-sensor technology and a built-in holographic projection unit that made the game look, feel, and sound like the actual invading aliens you had to actually fight were actually *in the room with you*. It came with two shiny silver zip-up motion-sensor bodysuits (so you could play with a friend) and a choice of motion-synchronized weapons: a TurboStaff, a BlasterShield, or a pair of MegaMittens. As you stood in front of the game, AlienSlayer:3-D! sensed your every move in the suit and with the weapons, allowing you to realistically battle the aliens. Every detail of the game was designed for a lifelike experience. As soon as you powered it up, whatever you were watching on TV—

cartoons, *Dancing with America's Most Talented Pets*, your dad's boring news show—would suddenly go all fuzzy, and suddenly you'd be face-to-face with LAZ-ROW, Evil Alien Overlord®, who'd announce:

"PEOPLE OF EARTH! WE INTERRUPT YOUR MINDLESS ENTERTAINMENT PROGRAMMING TO INFORM YOU THAT YOUR PLANET IS ABOUT TO BE INVADED—BY ALIENS!"

Then the holographic creatures would begin leaping out of your TV and start blasting away at you on your sofa.

With this game, Alex could have survived a hundred boring Merwinsville summers. But he'd made a promise. And his dad always said, "A promise is a promise"—although Alex never really understood why. A porcupine is a porcupine, too, but people don't go around saying that.

As Alex thought about all this stuff, his parents stood over him, grinning anxiously. Alex looked at the TV, closed his eyes, and pulled the trigger.

The very last Alien Invader squealed and exploded.

His mom and dad cheered and high-fived each other.

Alex sighed and heard what he'd been

dreading for weeks: "*CONGRATULATIONS, EARTHLING! YOU SLAYED THE ALIEN INVADERS, SAVED YOUR PLANET, AND SUCCESSFULLY COMPLETED ALIENSLAYER 2!... WATCH FOR ALIENSLAYER:3-D!, AVAILABLE IN STORES THIS SUMMER!*"

"Gee, thanks," Alex mumbled. "Now you tell me."

His dad gleefully yanked the game out of the back of the TV and started packing it up as his mother kissed him on the cheek.

"Honey, we're so proud of you. Not just for saving the planet, but for keeping your promise."

"That's right," his dad said, stuffing the boxed-up game onto the top shelf of Alex's closet behind his winter sweaters. "Because a promise is a promise."

"Here, sweetie," his mom said, handing him a folded-up T-shirt. "I made this for you."

Alex unfolded the T-shirt. Printed on the front in big, bold letters it said: *I ♥ SLAYING ALIENS*. Alex slipped it on and looked down at it. "Wow. You *really* shouldn't have."

"That's not *all* we shouldn't have!" his father said.

CHAPTER 2

"Surprise!" Alex stood in his backyard, staring at a brand-new, fully constructed, Safe-T-Kids Jump n' Jammin' Jungle Gym. It had a swing, a clubhouse, a climbing wall, and a ladder leading

up to the opening of a big, blue, spiraling tunnel-slide. Alex thought this could be really cool—if he could go back in time to when he was six years old.

"It's a jungle gym," he said.

"It's a *jungle gym!*" his mom repeated, only much louder.

His dad nudged him toward it. "Go on, son! Try 'er out!"

Alex slowly climbed the ladder. He sat at the gaping mouth of the tunnel-slide and looked down. His parents were beaming up at him like it was the greatest day of their lives. Inching forward, he slid through the dark tube, around the curve, and popped out the bottom, landing on the grass. His mom and dad stood over him with huge grins on their faces. "Oh," Alex remembered to say, "*whee.*"

His parents started high-fiving each other again, which was really beginning to annoy Alex. "I know you guys got this for me to help keep my mind off video games. And I appreciate it, but—"

"Stop right there, sweetie," Alex's mom said. "We know what you're going to say."

"You do?"

His dad chimed in. "Of course we do, champ. You can't have fun on this baby all by yourself!"

"Which is why we've arranged a playdate for you!" his mom grinned.

Playdate? Alex hadn't had a playdate since he was seven. And besides, he knew that his best friends, Henry, James, and Oliver, were all either away at sleepaway camp, on a family vacation, or grounded.

This was bad.

"Want a hint?" his mom teased. "It's someone who lives *very close by* . . ."

This was *really* bad.

POSSIBILITIES
FOR PLAYDATES:

Ellie   Sammi   Herbert

The list of potential playmates who
lived "very close by" included three terrible
possibilities. For starters there was Alex's little
sister, Ellie. She was extremely close by. In fact,
her bedroom was right across the hall from his.
Ellie was an okay little sister, but she was four.
Her idea of fun was putting dolly dresses on her
stuffed animals and then pretending to take
naps with them.

The second possibility was Sammi Clementine.
Sammi was Alex's age, and lived next door. Alex
had seen her racing in and out of her house all
summer, in a soccer uniform or a ballet tutu or a
karate *gi*. She was constantly being mini-vanned to
some rehearsal or tournament or divisional match.
Alex figured she must be pretty good at a lot of

stuff, since she did so much of it. He also figured she must be pretty cool. For a girl, anyway.

The last possibility was definitely the worst. Herbert Slewg was also Alex's age, and his neighbor on the other side. Herbert was a strange kid. He didn't have any friends that Alex knew of, but didn't seem to care. From what Alex could tell from hearing Herbert's mom yell at him all the time, Herbert enjoyed taking apart small appliances from her kitchen and putting them back together so they didn't work anymore. Alex had never really spoken to Herbert, but didn't think they'd have much to talk about—Alex wasn't interested in disassembling toaster ovens, and Herbert Slewg did not seem to be the video game playing type. Alex looked up at his mom and dad. They had Slewg written all over their faces.

Oh, no, Alex thought.

CHAPTER 3

Alex stepped up to the Slewgs' front door and rang the bell. Except it didn't ring. It *VROOMED.*

A small vacuum hose wearing fake nose-and-mustache glasses suddenly sprang out of a box just above the doorbell button.

"Hey!" Alex tried to jump back but was too slow—the sucker-nose pressed against his cheek. And *sucked.*

"What the *heck?!*" Just as quickly, the sucker-nose popped off his face and slammed back into its box. The front door opened, and a woman with a flippy hairdo stood smiling down at him.

"Alex!" Mrs. Slewg said sweetly. "I thought that smelled like you! Please, come in!"

Alex rubbed the red suction mark on his cheek as he stepped inside. Mrs. Slewg noticed.

"Oh, that was our *DoorSmell*," she explained. "Just another one of Herbert's inventions." She closed the door and pointed to a small vent on the wall. "When someone rings, the Nose-Hose

sniffs the caller, and a little whiff sprays in here.
If it's the pizza guy, it smells like pizza. If it's
the mailman, it smells like magazine perfume
samples. If it's you, it smells like, well—did you
have sausage for breakfast?"

Alex nodded slowly.

Mrs. Slewg cackled. "Herbert loves
sausage! Oh, you two are going to be
such good friends!"

She pointed down the hallway,
still chuckling. "Go on. His bedroom's
the last door, end of the hall. But
watch your head—I'm just about to finish my
housework!" Mrs. Slewg slammed a big, red
button marked HOUSEWORK and walked off.

WHOO-WHOO SPLAT! A train whistle made
Alex's head turn just in time to catch a cold, soggy
slap in the face. A dripping-wet pair of yellow-
ducky pajamas whipped past him down the hall.
They were suspended from a coat hanger.

The hanger was attached to a toy railcar, which sped along tracks stapled upside down to the ceiling. Every few seconds a damp sweater, soaked nightgown, or drenched bath towel barreled by in a caravan of wet laundry.

"Whoa!" Alex dove for the floor. A spinning metal hubcap wheeled along the rug, bounced off the opposite wall, and zoomed straight for his face. It had big scrubber-brushes attached to its outer edges, and a soap dispenser mounted on top. It squirted a glob of soapsuds into Alex's eyes as it sped toward him.

"Aaaaugh!" The spinning contraption nearly scrubbed his face off. Alex jumped up and quickly sat back against the wall as the crazed robo-rug scrubber bounced off his foot, shifted directions and slammed its way down the other side of the hallway.

Alex rubbed the soap out of his eyes as he heard a metallic *ROOOAAAAAAR!* from beside him. "What *now!?*" he yelped. A big, ugly, remote-controlled T-Rex dinosaur toy clunkily marched right at him. Duct-taped to its tiny arms was an electric kitchen mixer, which spun a pair of feather dusters instead of normal mixing wands. Its whirling, dust-filled feathery arms

blasted Alex's nose. He burst into a fit of sneezes and rolled away as the dino-duster continued to kick up dust bunnies all along the hallway wall.

"*Ow-tchoo!*" Alex

bumped his head against something as he let go one last sneeze.

He looked up. He never thought he'd feel so happy to see Herbert Slewg's bedroom door.

Scientific Experimentation in Progress.
DO NOT DISTURB, except in case of one
or more of the following emergencies:

Explosion (Gas, chemical, or hypothermal)

Extreme, observational, and/or
unearthly levels of bright light

Measurable temperatures above
1000°C or below 1000°C

Screams of pain, cries for help, or
unusually long periods of silence

Thank you,
H. Slewg, Inventor

Alex heard a loud zapping sound. Blue sparks
shot through the crack at the bottom of the door.
Alex checked this against the list, then knocked
anyway. The sparks stopped immediately.
The door flew open, and Alex nearly fell over.
Standing there was Herbert Slewg—wearing an
AlienSlayer:3-D! silver
zip-up bodysuit! In
one of his hands was a
small welding torch,
in the other was a
second suit. This was
too much for Alex.
Without thinking,
he leaped into the
room, slammed the
door behind him,
and snatched the suit

out of Herbert's hand. Herbert stared as Alex
frantically zipped up the suit over his clothes.

"Okay! I'm ready!" he said. He glanced around. "Where's the game? Where's the TV? *Where is AlienSlayer:3-D!?!*"

"Alex Filby, I presume," said Herbert.

Alex shook his hand quickly. "Yeah, hi. Look, I don't have much time. I came to bring you over to my place, but I'm not leaving here till I play your AS:3-D! game. So let's do this."

WHAT HA'

"The game isn't here," Herbert said. "Well, actually"—he pointed around the room to various, half-built gadgets—"it's here. And over there, and there's a little bit of it welded to that, there."

Alex picked up one of the odd objects. It was a TurboStaff, one of AS:3-D!'s wonderful weapons.

One end was broken open and spilling out wires like guts. The other was sloppily connected to the top of a living-room lamp, complete with a frilly, powder-blue lampshade. Alex's lower lip trembled slightly.

"As the sign says," Herbert explained calmly,

YOU DONE?!

"I'm an inventor."

"You're no *inventor*." Alex had a crazed look in his eyes. *"YOU'RE A MONSTER!"* Suddenly, Alex noticed something strange about Herbert's suit. He looked down at his own. Both were covered with wires, circuits, and lights. "What have you DONE?!" he said. "You've *changed* the motion-sensor bodysuits!"

Herbert gritted his teeth and squinted at this whining simpleton. His face grew red and blotchy.

"*Nice theory, Einstein*," he spat. "But no. I've *modified* them. I'm attempting to invent the world's first Negative Energy Densifiers, or N.E.D., suits, designed to enhance the molecular space between solid objects for the purpose of *physical transparency*." Alex just glared at him, so he decided to continue. "By working in tandem with the motion sensors preinstalled in the suits, my modifications will cause an object's molecular structure to negatively reconfigure at the exact moment of precontact, allowing the suit, along with its wearer, to pass through." Alex stared at him. There was a long silence. Somewhere far away, a dog barked.

"You ruined the coolest video game ever created," Alex finally whispered.

"*Video game?!*" Herbert scoffed. "My invention allows you to do in *real life* things that you could only pretend to do in your precious *video games*—

like walk through walls!" Herbert flipped a
switch on the belt buckle of his suit. The lights
flashed and the wires began to vibrate.

"Observe." Herbert turned, faced his bedroom
wall—and ran straight into it.

Almost immediately, Herbert popped up,
pulled out a tiny screwdriver and began making
adjustments to his suit. He stepped over to Alex

and quickly made the same adjustments. "Still working out some kinks," he said. "That should do the trick." Herbert stepped back and nodded toward the wall. "Go on. Fire her up and have a run at it!"

"Uh, no thanks," Alex said. "I think I'll just pass through the door, like normal people." Alex stepped out into the hallway and ducked back in, just in time to miss getting smacked in the face by a pair of Herbert's soggy underpants.

"C'mon," Alex said sadly. "Our moms are making us have a playdate together on my new jungle gym. We might as well get it over with."

CHAPTER

Alex sat atop the jungle gym ladder, at the mouth of the tunnel-slide, and watched as Herbert ran full-force into Alex's fence. He looked at Herbert rubbing his bruised head.

This "playdate" cannot get any worse, he thought.

Then he saw Sammi Clementine peeking over the fence separating his yard from hers.

"Hey, cool slide," she said.

"You betcha!" he blurted awkwardly. "Wanna come check it out? It's got a rock-climbing wall. I know you're into rock climbing. Tuesdays and Thursdays, noon to three, right?"

She looked at him. "Why would you possibly know that?"

Alex suddenly felt very warm, even though it wasn't very hot out.

"Anyway, I can't," Sammi said. "I've gotta get to my swim meet. I just heard something bump into my fence. I thought maybe you got a dog or something."

They both looked over at Herbert, who at that moment ran straight into a tree.

"Well, I'll let you guys get back to playing . . . spaceman, or whatever," she said. "See ya."

Sammi disappeared. Alex buried his face in his hands for a good long time. He heard a crunch as Herbert dove headfirst into a thick bush. He stared down at Herbert's blinking, lit-up N.E.D. suit, and studied his own suit: the lights, the wires, and the little switch on his belt buckle. Without thinking, Alex flipped it on. The lights went *BLINKA-BLINKA-BLINKA*.

The wires went HRUMMMMMMMM....It kind of tickles, he thought. Then he noticed a WUBBA-WUBBA-WUBBA . . . It was a strange, pulsing sound, and it wasn't coming from his N.E.D. suit. Something pulled at him. He turned. The sound was growing louder by the second—and it was coming from inside the slide.

A shimmering, silver-blue surface rippled and

vibrated a few feet down the tube, like a shiny electric curtain blocking the inside of the slide. Alex leaned in toward it and got a closer look. It was very weird, but not as weird as the fact that Alex wasn't leaning on purpose—*he was being pulled toward it.* Alex grabbed the edge of the tube slide. He looked back at Herbert, who was making adjustments to his N.E.D. suit with his tiny screwdriver.

"*Hey!*" Alex yelled.

Herbert looked up and saw that Alex's suit
was turned on. "Hey!" he barked back. "That is a
delicate piece of experimental equipment, which
you are *not* authorized to activate! Turn it off
immediately, before you break it!"

Alex didn't dare let go of his grip on the
tube to reach down and turn off his N.E.D. suit.
He was being pulled harder and harder every
second, and that *WUBBA-WUBBA-WUBBA* sound
was beginning to rattle the entire jungle gym.

"I said, turn it off!" Herbert was climbing the shuddering ladder toward Alex, holding his screwdriver in his teeth. With Herbert's every step, the force seemed to be pulling Alex harder and harder.

"Stop! Don't come any closer!" Alex yelled.

Herbert reached the top of the ladder and suddenly flew into Alex, as if yanked by some invisible force.

"What did you do?" Herbert yelled.

"Nothing!" Alex screamed back.

"Did so!"

"Did not!"

WUBBA-WUBBA-WUBBA-WUBBA-WUBBA-WUBBA!

The two of them were now side by side on their bellies, their feet dangling into the gaping, rattling mouth of the slide.

"The edge of the slide's too smooth—I can't hold on!" Herbert said through clenched teeth, the screwdriver still in his mouth.

"Try!"

"Great advice, thanks!"

"Shut up!"

"*You* shut up!"

WUBBA-WUBBA-WUBBA-WUBBA-WUBBA-WUBBA!! The awful noise echoed louder and louder inside the vibrating slide, as if it were some hungry monster whose stomach was grumbling harder because it knew it was about to be fed.

Alex and Herbert's faces were just inches apart.

Their fingers ached—and began to slip.

They *screamed*.

Herbert's screwdriver dropped from his opened mouth and clattered down the tube just before he and Alex let go.

FOOMP!

In an instant they vanished, swallowed up by the shimmering curtain of light. In the next instant, the light vanished behind them.

The jungle gym stopped vibrating immediately. At the bottom of the slide, Herbert's screwdriver skidded out and landed safely on the grass. Alex and Herbert, however, did not.

CHAPTER 5

CHAPTER 6

Alex popped out of the cave and skidded through the rocky dirt. His nose smooshed against something dirty, cold, and furry. It was resting on a large hairy foot, which was attached, predictably, to a large hairy leg. Alex slowly looked up. The large hairy foot and the large hairy leg were attached, not predictably at all, to a large hairy *caveman.*

Scrambling to his feet, Alex scurried back
toward the cave he'd just popped out of. But
instead of running into the cave entrance, Alex
ran *into the cave entrance*—it was there, but it
was solid black, painted on the wall of rock. He
slammed into it and bounced backward. Alex
quickly dived behind a nearby jungle fern.

Herbert was already hiding behind the fern,
crouched down, scribbling a long mathematical
equation in the dirt. Alex peeked through the
leaves, relieved to see that the caveman and his
cavemen buddies hadn't moved an inch. They
were gathered around a fire, so amazed with it
that they didn't seem to even notice the huge
woolly mammoth standing perfectly still,

staring at the fire with them. *What is wrong with
these guys?* Alex thought.

Alex looked at Herbert's scribbling. "What're
you *doing*? This isn't the time for homework!
I don't think it's even a time when homework
existed!"

Herbert didn't look up. "Quiet. I'm calculating
the probability of polarity-reversal within
hypothetical interdimensional time travel."

"*What?*" Alex whispered, glancing out at
his prehistoric pals. "Why don't you calculate
this, Brainiac—how the heck did my jungle gym
transport us to an actual *prehistoric jungle?!*"

"*Wormhole*," Herbert said.

Alex's eyes narrowed. "Call me that again," he said. "I dare you."

"I can't believe I didn't think of this!" Herbert said. "The built-in motion sensors in the video game suits, working in tandem with the molecular polarity enhancers I installed, stimulated previously unseen areas of exotic matter containing high quantities of negative energy density—the *exact* necessary conditions for a *wormhole!*"

Alex blinked at Herbert.

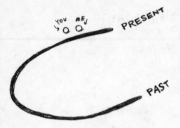

In the dirt, Herbert drew a horseshoe shape. "Observe. Einstein proved time isn't a straight line. It curves, like this. See? Present, past." He placed two pebbles on the "present" leg of the horseshoe. "These pebbles represent you and me."

Alex nervously glanced from the pebbles to the cavemen. "Okay. We're all just pebbles on the horseshoe of time. Got it. How 'bout we speed up the lesson?"

Herbert drew a line connecting the two legs of the horseshoe. "This is a wormhole. An invisible tunnel connecting two points in time."

"Like Chutes and Ladders!"

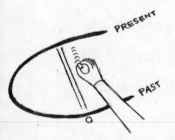

"Nice theory, Einstein. But no. My antimatter suits opened a wormhole in your jungle gym"— Herbert slid the Herbert and Alex pebbles from the "present" leg of the horseshoe to the "past" leg—"and safely transported us here, to what I'd estimate to be roughly 10,000 B.C."

"*Safely transported us?*" Alex forgot about the nearby cavemen for a moment. "Your stupid invention flushed us down the time-toilet!" he screamed. "We're stuck here!"

Herbert smiled. "Not to worry. My calculations lead me to conclude that reverse polarity can be achieved with our current negative energy displacement settings."

Alex gave him a threatening look.

"The suits," said Herbert. "They go in reverse."

Herbert and Alex tiptoed to the cave entrance. *TAP-TAP-TAP.* Alex knocked his hand against the fake, painted-on black cave entrance. Herbert nodded and hit the switch on his N.E.D. suit. It immediately lit up and hummed. The glowing, shimmery light from the tunnel-slide appeared in the painted-on cave entrance. Alex gave him a thumbs-up and hit his switch as well.

Nothing.

"Hold on a sec!" he whispered, glancing back at the woolly mammoth. "My thingy's busted!" He frantically flipped his switch on and off. "*Yo, pebble-boy! My thingy's busted!*"

Herbert was already getting pulled into the shimmering wormhole. He looked back at

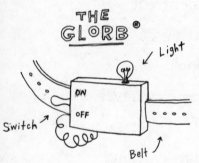

THE GLORB ®

Light

Switch

Belt

Alex and blurted, "Just jiggle the *glorb*—" as his head was swallowed.

"The *glorb?!* What the heck's a *glorb?!*" Alex saw Herbert's shoulders, then his back, sink into the wormhole. He glanced at the woolly mammoth—had it moved closer? He quickly turned back to Herbert and grabbed his ankles. He leaned back with all his might and yelled, "*No! This playdate is not over!*"

Alex put his
feet up on the side
of the rock wall
like a mountain
climber and tugged
backward. Slowly,
he started winning

OH NO —
YOU'RE NOT
LEAVING
ME
HERE!!!!

the tug-of-war with the wormhole! He could see
Herbert's knees, then his butt. Then he saw it.
Herbert's belt buckle.

"Eureka!" cried Alex. He hit the button that
shut off Herbert's N.E.D. suit. The wormhole
belched out Herbert and disappeared. Herbert
and Alex went flying backward. They sailed
through the air, slammed into a still-staring
caveman, and landed *in the fire.*

"Aaaaahhh!" they screamed together. "*Stop,
drop, and roll! Stop, drop, and roll!*" Alex and
Herbert held each other tightly as they rolled
around in the fire together. Eventually they

stopped. As the cavemen continued to stare at them, Alex and Herbert got up and checked themselves. Realizing that they weren't burned, burning, or even uncomfortably warm, they glanced down at the "fire" they'd just squashed. It was a bunch of red, yellow, and orange streamers being blown upward by a fan in the floor. And it *was* a floor. The sand, the fire, the cave, *it was all fake*. And if that was fake, then so were the—

CREEAAAAK!

Alex and Herbert looked at their prehistoric audience. One of the cavemen was moving. Well, *wobbling*. It wobbled like a department store mannequin—if a department store mannequin

46

were dressed up like a caveman, then slammed off-balance by two boys thrown through the air by a suddenly deactivated wormhole.

As Alex and Herbert watched, the wobbling cavemannequin stiffly fell over. *BONK!* It hit the cavemannequin next to it. *BONK!*—that one hit the next one. *BONK! BONK! BONK!* Like Neanderthal dominoes, they all toppled over one by one, until the last cavemannequin hit a boulder. Its head popped off and rolled to a stop at Alex and Herbert's feet. Alex glanced over at the woolly mammoth to get his reaction to all of this. The big, furry beast was now lying on her side, still staring at the trashed fake fire as if nothing had happened.

"Man, that's gotta be the most relaxed woolly mammoth I've ever seen," said Alex.

"It's not *relaxed*, it's inanimate." said Herbert. "All of this is."

Alex and Herbert slowly stepped back and

looked up at the "sky" above them. From this angle, they noticed something that would normally be hard to miss, if there weren't headless cavemen and relaxed woolly mammoths standing around to distract a person: A huge silver spaceship hovered over the entire scene.

"*Whoa,*" Alex said. He and Herbert took in the shiny flying saucer, and then read the large sign hanging nearby.

"I may have been a little off on the year," Herbert said. "But I stand by my theory."

12,000 B.C. • G'DALIENS INTRODUCE FIRE TO EARLY MAN!

CHAPTER 7

Herbert and Alex hopped a railing and stepped from the rocky sand onto a smooth, shiny black floor. They turned around and faced the very real-looking, but very fake, prehistoric scene.

"It's like a set from a movie!" Alex said. "About a bunch of cavemen and their pet woolly mammoth who are suddenly attacked by two kids from the future!"

Herbert stared at the spaceship above the scene, then looked down an endless hallway at hundreds of other stages, behind hundreds of other railings. "Except this isn't a movie set," he said. "It's some sort of museum."

Alex and Herbert walked across the hall and faced the next scene. Another spacecraft hovered, this time over an enormous glacier. A gigantic blow-dryer machine extended from an open hatch in the belly of the UFO. It was melting the ice. Mannequins of animals and humans were in various stages of being thawed out. "And we're not *from* the future," Herbert added, staring up at the UFO. "*I think we're in it.*"

The sign hanging from the spaceship over this diorama read:

11,000 B.C.: G'DALIENS RESCUE EARLY MAN FROM THE ICE AGE

As this sank in,
Alex and Herbert
were startled
by a voice from behind them:
*"WELCOME TO THE HALLWAY OF
HUMAN HISTORY!"* They spun around to see
a bubblelike silver sphere, about the size of a
beach ball, floating down the hall. A panel in its
metallic skin slid open, and it projected images
of excited schoolchildren crowding around and
pointing at the very prehistoric diorama Alex
and Herbert had just destroyed.

*"COME, STROLL DOWN THIS CORRIDOR OF
COOPERATION...."* the floating object continued.
*"MARVEL AT HUMANKIND'S HISTORICAL
HELPERS WHO HAIL FROM HIGH ABOVE THE
HEAVENS—THE G'DALIENS!"* The panel closed
and the words MONITORB MESSAGING flashed
across the sphere in an impressive and highly

53

memorable logo.

It began to replay its message as it drifted past Alex and Herbert. They looked at each other and thought the exact same thing, which didn't happen often: "What's a G'Dalien?"

Alex and Herbert strolled down the Hallway of Human History. Scene after mannequin-filled scene showed important moments in history and how humans, since the beginning of time, were given gifts, breakthroughs, and inventions from an unseen alien race known as *G'Daliens*. Whether it was the introduction of stone tools, the building of the pyramids, or the

WHAT'S A G'DALIEN?

invention of cheez-in-a-can, there was always a G'Dalien spacecraft hovering somewhere in the scene. It seemed that without G'Dalien help, humans never would have figured anything out. And yet, Alex and Herbert noticed that over the centuries, these helpful strangers always kept their distance and never showed themselves—that is, until the very last diorama in the Hallway of Human History.

It showed a G'Dalien spacecraft parked in the middle of a big city, surrounded by grateful, cheering humans who were overjoyed that these beings had saved their planet. It looked like a parade scene, with the humans holding

2050: G'DALIENS SAVE TWENTY-FIRST CENTURY MAN FROM GLOBAL SELF-DESTRUCTION AND MOVE IN PERMANENTLY.

PUSH TO PLAY

up babies, balloons, and banners that read,
WELCOME, G'DALIENS and *HOORALIENS FOR
THE G'DALIENS!* In the center of the hoopla,
apparently for the first time, the G'Daliens
had stepped out of their spacecraft and let

themselves be seen.

The G'Daliens looked—well, there's a saying that people say, which goes, *"If you can't say something nice, don't say anything at all."*

All right, fine.

The G'Daliens looked, to put it as politely as possible, *absolutely disgusting*. Their squidlike bodies were the color of moldy mushroom soup. They were fat and slimy with six legs, two shiny, ink-black eyes, and one small, lipless mouth crammed full of tiny, razor-sharp teeth.

"Ew," Alex said, staring at the fake alien's blobby belly. Then he heard something he'd never heard Herbert do before. *He was giggling.* "What?" said Alex.

"Look—" Herbert said through his growing giggles. "Look at his mustache!"

Alex looked at the slits that served as the G'Daliens' nose holes and burst out laughing. Perched directly beneath their fleshy nostrils were big, bushy, very obviously *fake* mustaches. But it didn't stop there. Alex pointed at something else. "*Look*—" he said, snorting out

SAY HELLO TO A G'DALIEN

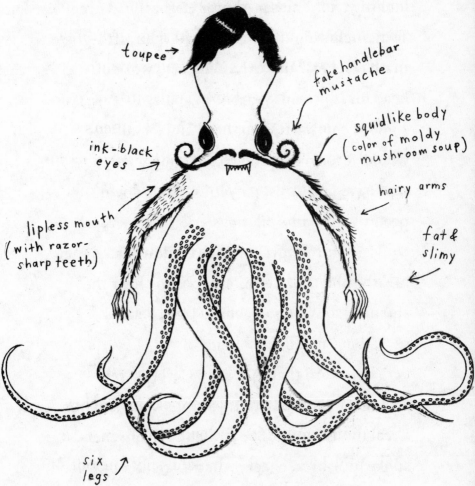

toupee →

fake handlebar mustache

squidlike body (color of moldy mushroom soup)

ink-black eyes →

hairy arms

lipless mouth (with razor-sharp teeth)

fat & slimy

six legs ↑

a laugh, *"Look at their hair!"* Indeed, resting like birds' nests on top of each and every G'Dalien mannequin's gray-green head was the silliest-looking *toupee* either Alex or Herbert had ever seen, including the squirrel-tail their fifth-grade math teacher, Mr. Kurlycheck, had worn on his head for last year's yearbook Faculty Picture Day.

This combination of head and facial hair would've looked strange on a human. On these repulsive creatures, they looked fall-down, pee-in-your-pants *hilarious*. Alex and Herbert couldn't stop laughing. They couldn't catch their breath. And they definitely couldn't hear the slurping sound approaching from behind.

"G'Day, mates!"

They heard that. Alex and Herbert spun around and looked up. Towering over them was a real live G'Dalien. She smiled at them, then spoke in a thick, cheery Australian accent. "Good onya, fellas, enjoying what's one of my favorite displays!" she gushed. "It's such a happy ending to such a come-good story, eh?"

She grinned at Alex and Herbert as she waited happily for a response. Alex and Herbert stood staring, frozen in fear.

CHAPTER 8

*T*he nastiest thing about seeing a real live G'Dalien in the flesh was, well, her flesh. It was grayish-green, like on the mannequins, but it was also kind of *see-through*. Like Jell-O, if Jell-O made a flavor called "Scummy Sewer Water." It wobbled like Jell-O, too. And when she chuckled, as CA-ROL suddenly started to do, the wobbling, scum-colored, semi-see-through Jell-O-like flesh was enough to make a person gag.

"No worries, boys," CA-ROL whispered. "I won't knock you two for sneakin' in before we're opened! You two eager-mcbeavers don't look like shonky bushrangers to me! It'll be our little secret, *fair dinkums?*" CA-ROL winked a large, glassy black eye at Alex and Herbert. Herbert didn't understand half the words that came out of her spike-filled mouth, but deduced from her accent that they were some sort of Australian slang. Alex thought for a second that her accented voice would've sounded quite nice if it weren't coming out of the jagged mouth hole of a horrifying alien squid-beast with a funny hairdo.

She turned to go, then suddenly spun back around. "Oh! I'm such a *drongo*—I almost forgot!" The boys squealed and flattened themselves against the diorama railing as her slimy tentacle shot past them and pointed to a large red button behind them. "This activates each historical scene—brings the past to life! G'day, fellas! Enjoy your day at the museum—and don't forget to visit the gift shop!"

Alex watched CA-ROL ooze off out of the hall. He looked from her trail of slime to Herbert's face. "That's it," he said. "I'm outta here."

"What?!" Herbert exclaimed. "We're in the future! Do you realize how much knowledge we can glean?!"

Alex yanked his arm out of Herbert's grasp. "Oh, I've gleaned, pal. I've gleaned that this is the future. And I've gleaned that in the future, Earth is *crawling with aliens!*" He turned and started down the hall again. "See you later," Alex said. "Or earlier. Or whatever."

Herbert looked at Alex carefully. "Okay. It's just a shame your suit is . . . *broken*."

Alex stopped. He looked down, then stepped up to Herbert, a little too close. "Give me yours," he said. Herbert took a step back, but Alex moved in closer. "You wanna glean some more with those octo-freaks? Stay and glean yourself silly. Just give me your suit, and I'll see you in a hundred years or so."

Herbert took another step back. "Tell you what. I'll repair your suit and we'll both go back together." he said. "All I ask is we take in one quick history lesson before we go." Herbert

nodded toward the big red button CA-ROL
had pointed out. "C'mon," he said. "I did not
travel one hundred years into the future at
approximately two-tenths the speed of light to
not learn *anything*."

C H A P T E R

9

As soon as Alex hit the button, he and Herbert jumped back. Music blasted from the diorama as the mechanized G'Dalien mannequins began to stiffly move, singing along to the very loud, very happy, and very annoying song.

Alex and Herbert looked above the robotic singers as the belly of a large spaceship lowered over the scene. A trapdoor opened. Out of it flew dozens of strange technological devices of all shapes and sizes.

The song ended as abruptly as it began. The mannequins snapped back to their original positions. The devices (attached by thin wires) were yanked back into the belly of the fake spaceship, which disappeared into the ceiling again.

"Wow, did I learn something," Alex said.

WHO KNEW THE FUTURE WOULD BE SO CHEESY?

Herbert had a look of delighted amazement on his face. "Do you realize what this means?" he whispered.

Herbert bolted out of the hall, past a sign that read *LOBBY/ENTRANCE*. Alex stood there a second.

Suddenly forced to choose between following Herbert or standing alone in an alien-filled museum with a broken time-travel suit, Alex made a quick decision. He caught up with Herbert in the vast museum lobby and immediately stopped running. Dumbfounded, he looked up.

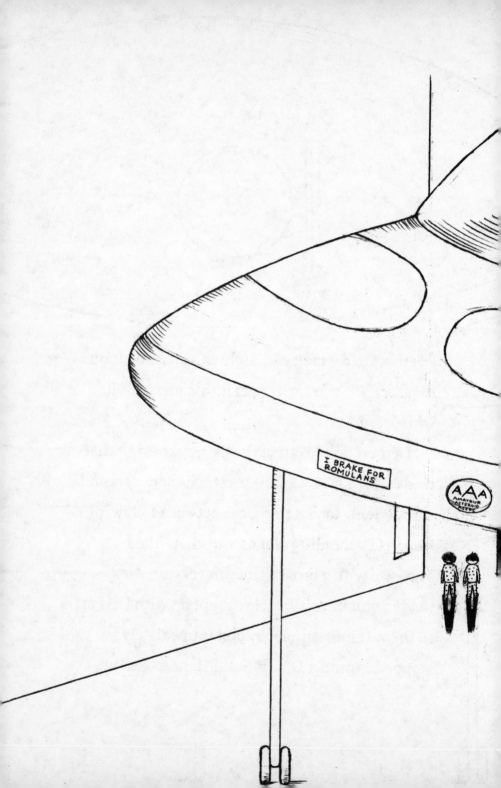

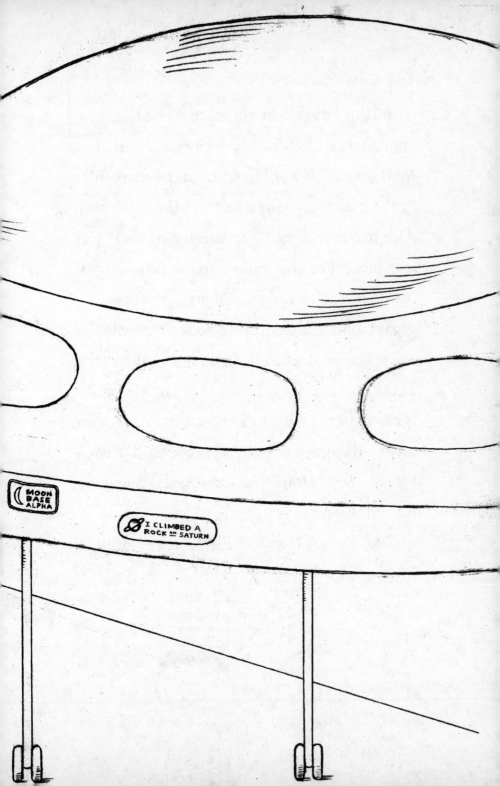

Filling the enormous space above the enormous lobby was an enormous G'Dalien MotherCraft. It was bigger than the spaceships in the dioramas—in fact, it was the biggest thing Alex had ever seen. He continued staring up at it as he walked and walked and walked—right into Herbert. Herbert stood just inside two gigantic museum entrance doors, each the size of a skyscraper. A *whoosh* of air blew in their faces as the massive doors began to open. Alex and Herbert stepped back as a soothing, Australian-accented voice suddenly filled the hall. *"G'day. Your attention please. The Merwinsville Museum of Human History is now open."*

"Did she say *Merwinsville*?" Alex breathlessly whispered.

They stepped through the open doors, out
onto the top of the museum's stone steps.

Spread out before them was twenty-second
century Merwinsville. The sky was so clear
and so blue it almost hurt to look at it. The
cityscape that stood up against this beautiful
blue backdrop was made up of incredibly huge
buildings. Giant football-shaped pods seemed
to balance on thin white legs that curved to
the ground. Clear transport tubes connected

CONCERT
IN THE
PARK
TONIGHT 8P

KEEP SMILING
SEE YOUR DENTIST

these structures, twisting and curving in
all directions. Between
the distant city and the
museum was a grove
of tall, green trees, like a little
forest connecting the plaza to
what looked like some sort of
archway entrance to downtown.
Alex and Herbert watched
in amazement as a large
rectangular object rose
from the distant edge of
the forest. It floated silently

toward the plaza and landed, as if on a cushion
of air. Alex and Herbert could read the writing
on the side of it as the door slid open noiselessly:
MERWINSVILLE ANTI-GRAVITRAM. Alex and
Herbert looked at each other. Their mouths hung
open, almost as wide as their eyeballs.

TAXI
GO METEORS
MERWINSVILLE ANTI-GRAVITRAM
MERWINSVILLE!!!
AS3D

They watched in amazement as a stream of humans and G'Daliens exited the tram together, spilling into the fresh, sun-drenched air.

In the Hall of Human History, a squatty G'Dalien in an orange vest angrily pushed a mop in front of his short, blobby body. His name badge read

GOR-DON. The G'DAY! part looked like it had been scribbled out with a black crayon, and his sour expression said, "Don't ask me *anything*." He looked down and spotted a pair of dirty footprints on the otherwise spotless floor. "*Ugh*," he muttered to himself. "Disgusting two-legged *apes*."

An extra *harrumph* shot out from beneath his bristly fake mustache as he dunked his mop into his bucket. He glanced up. The clatter of the mop handle hitting the floor echoed down the hall. GOR-DON's tiny, lipless mouth fell open. As he faced the destroyed caveman diorama, his inky-black eyes scanned the cluttered pile of mannequins along with the trampled, fake fire. GOR-DON looked back down at the footprints he'd been mopping up and followed them with his squinting, liquid-black eyes. The footprints led straight toward the lobby.

GOR-DON pushed the museum visitors aside as he rushed through the entrance door. He looked down at the clean white steps and saw more footprints. He spotted two humans as they reached the bottom of the steps and ran across the plaza toward the grove of tall trees that led to the city entrance. The angry G'Dalien squinted at their strange silver suits, shining in the sun.

His tiny mouth widened into an evil grin, revealing a pile of craggy, sawlike teeth.

"At least they'll be easy to track," he said.

CHA P TER

"See? You've got nothing to worry about." Herbert directed Alex's attention to the huge outdoor archway that towered above them. It was a giant statue of a smiling G'Dalien. Its six tentacles were stretched out, shaking hands with six humans. Their group handshake formed an arched gateway to the city. There were words carved in the stone:

FRIENDS FOREVER, REACHING ACROSS SPACE AND TIME. WELCOME TO MERWINSVILLE!

"See?" Herbert said. "Happy and friendly! No worries, mate!"

To Alex, the sculpted giant alien looked more like it was reaching out to grab a six-course meal. "If they're so happy and friendly, why do they look so nasty and creepy?"

"Who cares what they look like," Herbert said. "Look what they've given us!" Herbert and Alex stepped through the archway, onto Main Street, Merwinsville.

Except it wasn't really a street. It was more like

a giant sidewalk. An unbelievably clean, sparkling sidewalk, filled with unbelievably clean, sparkling storefronts, cafés, and restaurants. Dozens of MonitOrbs, like the one they saw in the museum, floated about in all different sizes; some filled the sky above them, while smaller ones drifted at eye level—transmitting public service messages, upcoming town events, and general happy thoughts for the day to the happy people and G'Daliens coming and going.

Weaving throughout the sky were clear transport tubes twisting like spaghetti in all directions overhead. But aside from that, there was no clutter in this city. There were no telephone wires. There were no trash cans. There was no *trash*.

"There are no cars," Alex said.

Herbert smiled back. "Who needs cars when you've got *those!?*" Alex looked up to where Herbert was pointing. Another Anti-GraviTram, like the one they'd seen land in front of the museum, drifted silently over the statue gateway and landed right in front of them. The doors slid open, and the citizens of Merwinsville began to disembark.

Every single commuter, whether human or G'Dalien, gave Alex and Herbert a hearty hello as they got off the tram. They chatted pleasantly with one another, whistled cheery tunes, or just plain smiled as they wandered off in different directions.

"See, I told you," Herbert whispered. "Friendly."

"No, I told *you*," Alex whispered back through a forced grin. "*Creepy.*"

Alex and Herbert watched as nearly all the commuters crossed the sidewalk and headed toward an area with a big sign that read

MERWINSVILLE TRANSPORTUBE STATION. On a large platform, dozens of clear tubes were lined up like a bunch of one-man, see-through elevator shafts. They all extended straight up, then each one curled and twisted off, over and across the city toward different destinations.

"Amazing," Herbert said as he approached the platform. "It appears to be some sort of individualized pneumatic transit system."

Alex's curiosity was beginning to overshadow his fear and disgust of the G'Daliens. "What, kinda like mini-wormholes?"

"Nice theory, *Einstein*," Herbert said as he closely watched an old man step toward one of the tubes. What little hair the old man had on his head suddenly stood straight up as the tube began making a gentle sucking noise. "But no," Herbert continued, "these appear to be more like—" *FOOMP!* In an instant, the old man was

sucked up the tube, twisting and turning as he
bulleted off somewhere in the city

"—*Crazy straws!*" Alex exclaimed. He leaped
onto the platform and lined up behind the
others. Herbert cautiously followed, watching
each Merwinsvillian go shooting off—*FOOMP!
FOOMP! FOOMP! FOOMP!*—one by one, in different
tubes, to different destinations. He noticed a
small suction cup device that shot out and stuck
to each traveler's forehead. A green light on the

tube would blink, and a soothing, computerized Australian voice would say, "Patrick's Surf Shop, 2307 Whelan Street" or "Charles Joseph Art Gallery, 342 Brentwood Avenue"—and the passenger would be instantly sucked away.

"Uh, hold up, Alex," Herbert said. "I'm not too sure about this—" But it was too late. Alex ran to the first available tube and stood beneath it. The suction cup popped out and stuck to his head. The light blinked red. "Transport denied," it said.

"Unable to access I-DNA data in Global Directory. Please exit TransporTube. G'day!"

"*What?!*" Alex yelled at the tube. "That's *so* not fair!"

"C'mon." Herbert quickly ushered Alex out of the tube and off the platform, away from the other waiting commuters. "We'll walk."

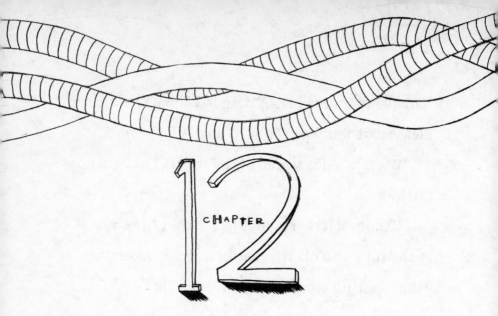

CHAPTER

12

Herbert and Alex made their way down the spotless walkstreets. "I wonder where everyone is," Herbert said.

"They're all up *there*," Alex moped, pointing above them. He was right. High above their

heads, the tangle of clear tubes was filled with people whooshing by, on their way to wherever they were going. "I don't get why we can't ride the

tubey thing. We lived here first—
a whole *hundred years* before any of these—"

"*Will you shush it!*" Herbert snapped, turning
to Alex. "We don't know how people will react if
they find out we're from—*the past.*"

"Oh, relax. Who's gonna hear me, the dogs, or
their robo-walkers?" Alex pointed out practically
the only other living creatures sharing the giant
sidewalk with them—dogs of all shapes and sizes,
with leashes attached to what looked like miniature
doughnut-shaped spaceships. They had blinking
lights and antennae on them, and they floated
along a few feet off the ground as they held the
ends of the dogs' leashes. One of the dog-walking
doughnuts stopped in front of Alex. A tiny door
opened, and a mechanical arm extended, holding
a small baggie. Alex rudely pushed it out of the
way. "Hey, I'm walking here!" he said. It bobbled in

midair as he nudged it aside and stepped—

SQUISH. Alex looked down. The robo-walker's dog, a furry Labradoodle, was staring up at him apologetically. "Oh, great." Alex said, lifting his shoe. "This would never have happened if we'd taken the tube." The robo-walker steadied itself and drifted back to its responsibilities. As the mechanical arm scooped up the poop *not* stuck to Alex's shoe, another door opened and a little sprayer-hose popped out. It blasted Alex's feet with water. "Hey!" Alex exclaimed, then realized what it was doing. "Oh. Er, thanks."

As they got deeper into the heart of downtown Merwinsville, they saw fewer dogs being walked, and saw more residents. On every street corner and in front of every major place of business, there were TransporTube booths. As Alex and Herbert passed them—*FOOMP! FOOMP! FOOMP! FOOMP!*—transported Merwinsvillians arrived at their destinations, looking happy and relaxed, but with their hair standing straight up on end. Conveniently, attached to the side of each booth was a domed, helmet-shaped object.

Alex and Herbert watched as one woman stepped out of the TransporTube booth, her long blonde hair jutting out like she had a giant sea urchin on her head.

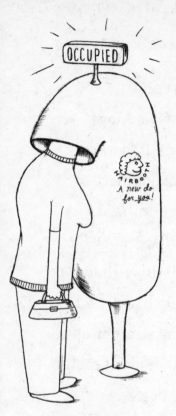

She stepped to the helmet and stuck her head in it. A light blinked, and the dome beeped. She pulled her head out, her hair perfectly combed, curled, and coiffed. There was even a tiny bow in it. She smiled at Alex and Herbert, then turned and entered a nail salon.

"Fascinating!" Herbert rushed to the hair-helmet and studied it, careful not to put his head inside. "I wondered how they'd offset the inevitable side effects of static electricity. *Genius!*"

More residents also meant more G'Daliens. "G'day!" said one tall and skinny extraterrestrial. He tipped his toupee as he passed, but Alex just stared back at him suspiciously, careful not to turn his back on him. When it was safe, he looked at Herbert, who was still gleefully inspecting the hair-helmet. "Look at you," Alex said bitterly. "Here we are, totally surrounded by alien slimebags, and all you're interested in are these stupid *inventions*. You're happy as a pig slopping around in the mud."

"I suppose I am," Herbert said. He stood and faced Alex. "If by 'pig' you mean scientist, and by 'mud' you mean technological miracles."

"They're *aliens*," Alex said.

"Benevolent aliens."

"Trust me, there's no such thing."

"You play too many video games."

"Oh yeah?"

"Yeah."

They turned to face a boy about their age. He was wearing jeans, a T-shirt, a baseball cap—and a very amused grin.

WHAT'S WITH THE ALUMINUM UNDERWEAR?

Alex and Herbert glanced down. In their N.E.D. suits, they looked like a pair of walking Hershey's Kisses. Alex thought quickly. Too quickly. "Uh, laundry day?"

"We're not from around here," Herbert chimed in. "Because we're from, er, somewhere else."

"Yeah, I guessed," the boy said. "That's cool. Not your outfits. Those are very, very *not* cool. I just mean, I hardly ever get to meet anyone from somewhere else." He stuck out his hand. "Name's Chicago. Chicago Illinois. How'd you guys like a tour of the most boring town of all time?"

Alex and Herbert smiled at each other, and followed Chicago, Illinois.

As they made their way through downtown Merwinsville, a MonitOrb followed them. It was unusually large for a street-level sphere, and was showing one of many *Gladvertisements:* streaming video images of very happy humans with very happy G'Daliens doing very happy things, produced by something called the Department of Human/G'Dalien Harmony Enforcement, whose logo was prominently displayed in the bottom corner of the production.

The other curious thing about this particular MonitOrb was that even though it was effortlessly floating along, it appeared

to have feet—or rather, *tentacles*. Six of them.
As the sphere began to show video images of
humans and G'Daliens playing Frisbee in a park
with a golden retriever, GOR-DON peeked out
from behind it. The MonitOrb he had in his grip

suddenly blasted happy, cheery music, startling him. GOR-DON fell down and was clunked in the head by the video-sphere as it drifted past him and rose back into the air. Landing on his blobby butt, GOR-DON squirmed like an overturned turtle. A passing troop of helpful human girls in StarScout uniforms rushed to help him up, but GOR-DON pushed them aside. "Get away from me!" he snarled. Then he stole their cookies and oozed off to continue his undercover pursuit of the two silver-suited humans.

CHAPTER 13

Chicago pointed to a strange-looking building. It was basically a moon-sized, see-through bubble sitting atop a single long white leg. "That's City Hall," he said.

"It looks like a giant golf ball on a tee," Herbert said. The ball had dozens of clear TransporTubes connected to it, and they could see G'Daliens being pumped in and out of it.

"A golf ball full of slugs," Alex added. He could see hundreds of G'Daliens inside the transparent golf ball, working and bustling around, like slimy bees in a hive. *Evil, plotting slimy bees*, he thought to himself.

"The G'Daliens run the whole city from up there," Chicago said. He suddenly stopped walking and smacked himself in the head. "Oh, no!" he said. "That reminds me—I've got school today!"

"Uh, okay." Herbert said awkwardly. "We understand."

"Do you guys mind waiting?" Herbert and Alex glanced at each other. "Cool!" Chicago said. He stepped over to a head-sized cone mounted to a post and stuck his head inside of it. Display lights flashed. The cone made a school-bell sound. Chicago popped his head out.

"Sorry that took so long—I had three tests, a ton of reading to download and a mental report due." Alex and Herbert smiled. "Okay! On to our next stop."

The First National Memory Bank looked like an ordinary bank, if banks were run by squidlike aliens. It had a wall of ATM machines and a walk-up counter of G'Dalien bank tellers. From a comfortable distance, Alex watched one of them greet an old woman with an Australian-accented "G'day, ma'am!" The teller slapped one of her tentacles onto the old woman's forehead and immediately seemed to know all about her.

"Mrs. Nebraska! Nice to see you again! Enjoy your visit with the grandkids last month, didja?"

"Oh, it was a wonderful trip, thank you," the woman said, completely at ease with having a slimy tentacle flopping in front of her nose.

"I'll bet those little ankle-biters are getting

bigger by the second," the G'Dalien said. "Now, how can I help you today?"

"Well, I can't seem to remember where I put the cat."

"I'm sure Little Fluffernutter is safe and sound. Now, let's have a quick looky-loo." The G'Dalien stared off for a few seconds, then suddenly blurted out, "Aha! Looks like you accidentally mailed that furry little roo to your sister Rita again. And I think you'll find the sweater you knit her for her birthday in the litter box. Now, is there anything else I can help you with today?"

"No, thank you so much," she said.

POP! The teller yanked her tentacle off Mrs. Nebraska's head. "Alrighty! G'day, then, Mrs. N!" She looked past her to the line. "Next!"

Alex looked terrified as he watched Mrs. Nebraska shuffle past him with a relieved smile on her face and a red mark on her forehead. He rushed over to Herbert, who was lying on the floor, inspecting the underbelly of one of the ATM machines. "Hey! Curious George! We gotta get out of here! This is not a normal bank!"

Herbert sat up and gave him a look. "This is not a normal bank. Take a look at these ATM machines!" Alex looked at the top of the machine. *ATM* stood for *Access-Transferable Memories*, and the one Herbert was studying was designated *WITHDRAWALS ONLY*. Herbert leaned his head toward the screen. A suction cup shot out and stuck to Herbert's forehead.

Alex grabbed Herbert's hair and yanked. "This is just like Human Zombies: Global Mind-Control 3! Quick! Clear your head—*think about baseball!* Or else the aliens will suck everything out of your brains and replace it with freaky gibberish!"

NOOo!!!

Herbert smacked Alex's hand away. He spoke in a dazed voice. "It's . . . an open-source temporal portal to a synapse-based data-retrieval system . . ."

Alex stepped back, horrified. "I'm too late. . . . The transformation has begun."

POP! The suction cup snapped back into the machine. Herbert looked at Alex with a dazed grin.

"Are you okay? Say something!"

Herbert smiled. "That thing just downloaded *gigabytes* of general knowledge into my prefrontal cortex! The city's layout and cultural history, movie and restaurant reviews—Hey! Andretti's Pizzeria is *still* over on Seaver Street! Oh, and we need to come up with place names for ourselves—most people our age are named after where their ancestors were born. And wait till you see the—"

"*All right!*" Alex snapped. "I get it! You're still *way* smarter—and might I add, *annoyinger*—than me!" He stepped over to the next ATM machine. "Well, stand back, Smarty McShinyPants. Because now it's *my* turn to get me some gigglebites."

Herbert glanced up at the machine Alex was suddenly jamming his head into, and his eyes grew wide. "No, wait!" he cried.

THWAP! The suction cup hit Alex's head, and the machine hummed to life. A minute later it popped back off and Alex stumbled back.

Herbert looked at him. "You okay?"

"I think so. Don't feel any smarter, though."

"No, I wouldn't think you would." They both looked at the top of Alex's ATM machine. It said, *DEPOSITS ONLY.*

"Uh-oh," Alex said.

"Think," Herbert said. "What memories did you deposit?"

"I don't know. I can't remember."

"Okay. Don't panic."

Alex thought hard, then finally said, "What the heck's a video game?"

Herbert stared at Alex. Chicago appeared

behind them. He had a big red suction mark on his forehead. "All set—" he stared at them for a few seconds, as if he were trying to remember something. "I just realized I forgot to ask you guys your names."

"Oh! I know this one," Alex said. "My name's Alex—"

"—*Ville!*" Herbert quickly added. "He's Alex*ville*. And I'm—"

"—*Herbalulu.*" Alex grinned.

"Okay, Alexville and Herbalulu. You guys like pizza? I know this great old place over on Seaver Street, called Andretti's."

Alex stared at Chicago. "Wow. It's like you just read my mind."

As they exited the bank, a skinny man stepped up to the ATM Herbert had used. He was suddenly hip-checked across the room by a large blobby butt. "Pardon me," GOR-DON hissed.

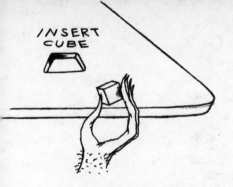

INSERT
CUBE

"But I believe I was next." He inserted a small green cube into a square hole in the ATM. It began to glow.

The three boys made their way across town, with Herbert happily using his brand-new downloaded knowledge of the city to advise Chicago on a more efficient way to get to Andretti's Pizzeria. Alex followed them, studying the mixed-species crowd. For some reason, the G'Daliens didn't scare him anymore. He caught up to Herbert and quietly spoke to him as they continued walking.

"It's so weird," Alex said as they passed a group of G'Daliens in business suits on their lunch hour. "Earlier today, I'd have slowed down to walk behind you when I saw one of those wobbly dudes coming toward me—hoping that it'd eat you first and be too full to chase me."

"I see," Herbert said.

"But since we left the Memory Bank, it's like I can't remember why I was ever afraid of aliens in the first place."

"That *is* weird," Herbert said, trying not to smile. "Maybe they *brainwashed* you."

Alex considered this. "Maybe." He shrugged. "But it's really not so bad."

Andretti's Pizzeria was one of the few good things about Merwinsville back in Alex and Herbert's time. It had the best pizza in town—at least, it did back at the start of the twenty-first century. And that, Alex and Herbert figured, must be the reason it was chosen above all others

as a historical building and preserved for a
hundred years.

"Can you believe Andretti's is still here?"
Herbert whispered to Alex as they approached

the familiar-looking pizzeria.

"It's like a beautiful dream wrapped in a happy fairy tale," Alex said, "then stuffed inside a cheese-filled calzone."

"I wonder if they kept the giant pizza oven."

"And if my high score is still on the—" Alex looked off, trying to remember something. "What was that machiney-thing, over by the bathroom, where you'd put money into it and get a score?"

"Soda machine?" Herbert asked innocently.

"Yeah." Alex said. "It'll be cool to see if my high score is still there on the soda machine."

Chicago reached the restaurant first and opened the door for Alex and Herbert. "Welcome to Andretti's, guys. Some of my teammates should be here already. I can't wait for you to meet them."

Alex and Herbert stepped inside.

"The pizza oven's gone," Herbert said.

"And where's the soda machine?" Alex asked.

"At least the booths are still here."

"Yeah, but I don't remember them *flying*."

The red leather booths attached to round tables were all that was left inside Andretti's.

There was no counter, no kitchen, no oven, no video games near the bathroom, no *bathroom*. Just the booths attached to the tables. Each one was packed with kids, and they were all hovering a few feet off the floor, flying around the restaurant, slamming into one another.

"What's the matter with you guys? You look like you've never been to a bumper-car pizza place before." Chicago looked across the room and exclaimed, "There are my buddies—c'mon!"

Alex and Herbert watched as Chicago ran

across the middle of the restaurant, which in this particular restaurant was extremely dangerous. He dodged speeding bumper-booths, leaped over one table, grabbed the back of a red leather booth, and hopped into it as it zoomed by. As it spun and sped past a stunned Alex and Herbert, Chicago yelled, "Hop on!"

"I suddenly find that I'm not that hungry," Herbert muttered.

"Who cares?" Alex replied. "This is *so cool!*" Alex grabbed Herbert's hand and yanked him out onto the floor.

"*Aaaaah!*" Herbert screamed as he and Alex dodged and weaved past colliding booths, just missed getting slammed, and finally leaped for Chicago's red leather banquette.

A thick arm pulled both of them up, and a skinny arm quickly buckled them in. The arms belonged to two of Chicago's best friends, as

Chicago explained when he introduced them. Dallas was a big kid with a buzz haircut, bulky muscles, and a constantly confused look about him. Sausalito was a tall, skinny kid with longish hair that flopped over sleepy eyes. He wore a goofy grin and music earbuds with antennae sticking out of them. Alex thought he looked like a very relaxed insect.

As their booth bounced off the far wall, Herbert and Alex knocked heads. "EL-ROY, watch

where you're steering!" Chicago said. "Oh, and say hello to Alexville and Herbalulu."

"G'day, fellas!" shouted a tiny voice from a tiny head that barely peeked over the tabletop. EL-ROY was a young, very short G'Dalien. He hopped back onto his booster seat and regained control of the big, silver pizza-tray holder in the center of the table. He spun it, and the booth veered around a group of kids by the door waiting for a table.

Herbert smiled hello to EL-ROY. Alex grinned and blurted out, "You don't creep me out, and I can't remember why!"

The G'Dalien waiter suddenly bounced up
to their table and latched on. He spun a giant
slab of raw pizza dough over his head as they
all slammed around
the room.

> I'M TOTALLY COOL WITH THIS!

Without
saying a
word, he shot his
other arms out and
popped a
tentacle on
each of the boys' heads.

"I'm totally cool with this!" Alex said
from behind the fat alien-arm dangling in front
of his nose. The waiter mind-read their favorite
topping, popped his tentacles off their heads,
and flipped ingredients out of his apron pockets
onto the still-spinning pizza dough.

As the booth bounced off a wall, the G'Dalien

waiter calmly pulled out a very dangerous-looking laser-wand and scanned it over the dough. He dropped the piping hot pizza on top of the silver wheel and then leaped to another table to brain-suck another order.

"I love this place!" Alex suddenly yelled out. Alex was feeling good. It was the feeling-good kind of good feeling anyone might get if they were about to share their favorite pizza in the whole world with a bunch of new friends. The only thing was, when Alex was feeling this good, he got chatty. And when he got chatty, he made stuff up. And Alex was feeling *really* good.

"So," Dallas asked, grabbing a slice, "are those silver suits, like, A.G. T-Ball uniforms or somethin'?"

"T-ball?" Alex said. "Why yes. Yes they are."

"So why are they all . . . silver and stuff?" Dallas probed further.

"Well, obviously they're professional grade," Alex confidently fibbed, "which is as it should be, since Herbalulu and I are professional T-ball players."

Chicago and EL-ROY looked up from their pizza. "You guys are Level One Certified?" the little G-Dalien squeaked.

Alex nodded proudly as he held up his sleeve. "Check out this material. Of course we are!" He felt Herbert kick him under the table and ignored it.

"Awesome!" Chicago said, "We need two players for tomorrow's game!"

"Well, then this is your lucky day," Alex smiled, "because we happen to be two players who are awesome."

High fives broke out around the table. Alex smiled and did his best to ignore Herbert, who glared at him.

"You guys are saviors!" Chicago said. "We've got a game against the Thrashers at noon tomorrow and I've got two guys out with head injuries!"

CHAPTER 15

*E*veryone stepped outside of Andretti's, dizzy but excited. That is, everyone but Alex and Herbert—they were dizzy and concerned. "So guys," Alex asked sheepishly. "We *are* talking T-ball, here. Little ball sits on a little tee, you walk up, hit it, go around the bases, right?"

"That's the game, mate—*no worries!*" EL-ROY chuckled. Dallas slapped Alex on the back, way too hard.

"This dude is funny!" Dallas blurted. "He's

a funny dude!" They all laughed together. Alex shrugged to Herbert and forced a laugh. Herbert wasn't laughing.

"I've gotta tell my dad about you guys," Chicago said. He squeezed the rim of his baseball cap. "I'm team captain, but he's the coach." A small antenna popped out of the top of Chicago's cap and emitted a tiny beep before disappearing back inside. He nodded up at the sky. "He should be right down."

Alex and Herbert squinted up at the sky. High above, they could barely make out a tiny black dot. It looked like a birthday balloon that had escaped the party. *WHOOSH!* In less than a second, the black object was right in front of them. But it wasn't a dot—hovering above the street was a sleek, black flying car with words printed on its side: *DEPARTMENT OF HUMAN/ G'DALIEN HARMONY ENFORCEMENT.* The door lifted open like a batwing and a man with a thick mustache stepped out. He was wearing a trench coat and an old-timey hat. He looked around very seriously, like he was expecting trouble, or hoping to find it.

"Hey, Pop!" Chicago said. As soon as he spotted Chicago and his friends, the man's face lit up. He gave his son a hug. Then he stepped over to Dallas and EL-ROY.

"Hey, how are you two getting along?" he asked with some suspicion.

"Great!" Dallas said.

EL-ROY smiled. "No worries, Mr. I!"

Mr. Illinois seemed a little disappointed to hear this. As Dallas, EL-ROY, and Sausalito said their good-byes and headed off, laughing and talking together, Mr. Illinois sighed.

"Good kids. Never any trouble. Not even a little." He suddenly called after them. "Well, you be sure to report any trouble, or let me know if you're not, y'know, getting along, okay?"

"Why wouldn't they get along?" asked Alex.

Mr. Illinois spun around and faced Alex and Herbert. "Exactly who are you two?" he asked.

EXACTLY WHO ARE YOU TWO?

"Dad, meet Alexville and Herbalulu," Chicago said. "They're Level One Certified! They're gonna fill in tomorrow!"

Mr. Illinois squinted at them slowly and carefully. "I've got a keen eye," he finally said. "And two things tell me you guys are good—my gut . . . and your shiny suits." He smiled and offered his hand. "Welcome to the team, boys. Springfield Illinois–Human/G'Dalien Harmony Force. You two troublemakers?"

"No, sir," Herbert said.

"Good," Mr. Illinois said, sort of sadly. "That's what we, y'know, like to hear."

131

The other batwing door whooshed open and the floating car lifted about another foot. Out stepped the biggest, fattest G'Dalien Alex and Herbert had seen so far.

"Don't mess with me, LO-PEZ," Mr. Illinois barked. "I'm not in the mood."

"I'm not messin', Sarge." said LO-PEZ. "Just came in, and we're the only ones on duty."

Mr. Illinois slowly walked over to LO-PEZ. He stared at his extra-large partner, then suddenly burst into a big grin. He hugged him and jumped up and down, like he'd just won the lottery.

"Dad?" Chicago said. "Shouldn't you, y'know, *go?*"

Mr. Illinois looked back at them with tears of joy in his eyes. "Hey! Why don't you guys come along! We haven't had a call to check out in years! Who knows if this'll ever happen again!"

The enormous LO-PEZ looked like he'd been poured into the tiny driver's seat. His blobby alien-flesh smooshed against the windows and drooped onto the floor. But his six arms were a blur: hitting buttons, pulling levers, steering, accelerating, adjusting the air conditioner—all while eating a bag of chips.

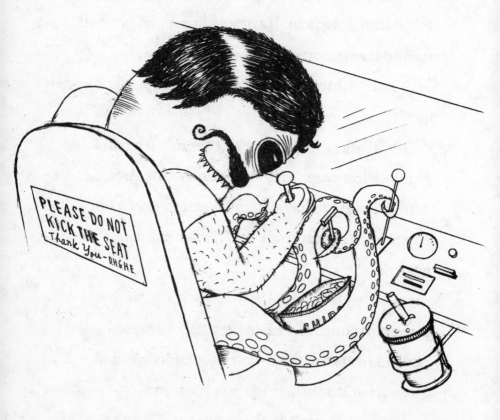

"I think I'm gonna be sick," Herbert mumbled to Alex. Herbert, Alex, and Chicago were jammed in the tiny backseat.

"*Don't*," Alex shot back without looking up from the floor. "If you hurl, your chunky puke will mess up my view!"

Beneath their sneakers, the floor of the SquadCar was see-through. Alex was amazed as he watched the tops of the huge, G'Dalien-designed orb-buildings whiz by below. Herbert couldn't look. He was too nauseous.

Mr. Illinois turned around in the passenger seat. "Okay, boys, here's what we got. A G'Dalien janitor called in a disturbance up at the Museum of Human History. Says he saw two young humans '*vandalize*' one of his exhibits." Alex and Herbert glanced at each other. Alex's amazement vanished. Herbert's nausea quadrupled.

CHAPTER

"Securing drop-corridor," Mr. Illinois said as
LO-PEZ hovered the SquadCar high above the
museum. Alex looked down through the floor
at the massive plaza a thousand feet below and
tried to figure out what the little gray spots were,
gathered in front of the museum steps.

"Goin' down!" LO-PEZ suddenly exclaimed,
slamming a button with his tentacle. Alex
thought the button somehow controlled his
stomach, because it immediately tried to leap out

of his throat. The AirCar dropped, and in a split-second those tiny spots a thousand feet below him were suddenly huge G'Daliens, right outside his door.

Alex and Herbert pretended to follow Chicago, his father, and LO-PEZ as they waded through the crowd gathered before the museum steps. "We'd better stay back, just in case things get ugly," Herbert said. They hid behind the squad car.

"Look at all these G'Daliens," Alex noted. "How could it get any uglier?" He and Herbert

climbed on top of the
SquadCar and stayed low.
Still, they could see over
the heads of the crowd a
mean, somewhat upset-
looking G'Dalien on the
museum steps, standing
beside a bucket and a mop.
It was GOR-DON.

"For fifty years I've worked in this museum,"
GOR-DON said to the gathered crowd. "Day
in and day out, cleaning, dusting, and
mopping every inch of a wretched building
dedicated to the wretched history of a wretched
species—*humans.*"

A massive gasp rose from the G'Dalien crowd. "Oh, *please!*" GOR-DON snapped. "You all know as well as I do that humans are an inferior species—*It's why we had to come here, remember?!*"

GOR-DON's left eye twitched as he stared out at the blank faces in the crowd.

"Can anyone tell me why we help humans, anyway? They're an untrustworthy, self-centered, fickle bunch who don't deserve us! We give them everything, and they just take and take and take, and then they have the nerve to tell us we're *'emotionally unavailable'*? Well, here's a news flash. I'm not human, *okay?* Maybe my 'emotions' *are* available, but you just don't know how to read them, because they're so much more advanced than yours will ever be! Did you ever think of *that, Marion?!*"

MARION?

YEAH, THAT'S THE ONE. WORKS IN THE CAFETERIA. NICE LADY.

GOR-DON suddenly stopped his rant and looked out at the crowd. They stared back at him with puzzled looks on their faces. "Well, I for one am tired of dumbing myself down just to make humans more comfortable. *We are the advanced race! We shouldn't be helping them, we should be enslaving them! It is time for all G'Daliens to rise up and show their true faces!*"

GOR-DON suddenly reached up and pulled his toupee off. Then he yanked the furry fake mustache from his upper lip. The crowd gasped and went silent. GOR-DON held his facial hair high above his suddenly nubby, bald head. His beady black eyes welled up with tears. His lip trembled. He shrieked in pain. *"Owwweeee!!!"*

Alex and Herbert watched from the roof of the SquadCar behind the crowd, kind of enjoying the show.

"Bad idea," Herbert said.

Alex frowned. "I dunno. It kinda makes him look younger."

GOR-DON frantically tried to blow air from his nose holes onto his raw upper lip. The crowd burst out laughing at him.

"You got serious issues, mate!" a G'Dalien in the crowd yelled out. "Humans wouldn't harm a Bhorarmian dust mite!"

"Yeah!" his buddy yelled,

"And why would we listen to a janitor, anyway? Especially one without a *mustache!*" The mob laughed louder. Even Chicago, Mr. Illinois,

and LO-PEZ shared a chuckle in the middle of the crowd. GOR-DON seethed as he looked out at them all. He reached a tentacle into his bucket and held high in the air something that immediately shut everyone up—*a human head.*

SWEET CHARIOTS OF FIRE!

"That G'Dalien has *beheaded a human!*" Mr. Illinois exclaimed. "LO-PEZ! Call for backup! I'm going in!" In an instant, Mr. Illinois broke through the crowd and dive-tackled GOR-DON.

"*Ghaaaak!*" the G'Dalien yelled, tossing the head into the air. He and Mr. Illinois rolled down the steps in a tangle of arms, legs, and tentacles, stopping at the foot of the mob.

Mr. Illinois sat up on top of GOR-DON and shoved a shiny badge in his face. "*Department of Human/G'Dalien Harmony Enforcement!*" he hollered. "You're under arrest, Freakshow! For— uh, *unauthorized and highly inharmonious removal of a person's head!*" The tossed head plopped onto the pavement in front of the crowd and split open, revealing itself for what it was—the fake, hollow caveman head from the museum. Mr. Illinois snapped on rubber gloves. He picked it up and studied it like a true detective. Then he looked up at the crowd. "Sorry, folks. My mistake. Nothing to see here."

"Get off me, you idiot!" GOR-DON yelled. He pushed Mr. Illinois to the side and staggered to his feet. "You see?!" he yelled to the crowd, "Humans are a *stupid, inferior, violent species!* This morning two of them destroyed this exhibit! And they're not alone! They're soldiers in some sort of—of *secret army,* sent here to kill our kind! And they're organized—they wear identical *silver battle uniforms!"*

Hearing this, Mr. Illinois and LO-PEZ glanced at each other. Chicago looked back. The crowd turned around, too, and cleared a path all the way back to the SquadCar . . . where Herbert and Alex were standing on the roof.

Herbert started to stuff his N.E.D. suit up his shirt and was doing a terrible job of blocking Alex from the crowd's view. "Hey, what's everybody looking at?" he said.

Alex finished stuffing his N.E.D. suit down his pants and stepped out. "Yeah," he said.

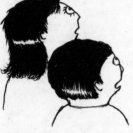

The crowd gasped. Herbert glanced at Alex, and his face dropped. Alex looked down. In giant block letters, his T-shirt read, *I ♥ SLAYING ALIENS.*

A short G'Dalien stepped forward with a camera. *SNAP!* He took their picture and slid back into the silent crowd.

"Seize them!" GOR-DON shrieked.

Alex and Herbert dived back inside the SquadCar and slammed shut the batwing doors.

Alex frantically stabbed buttons and pulled levers. Herbert grabbed Alex's suit from out of his pants and started messing around with its wires and sensors. "Head for the museum!" he yelled.

The SquadCar suddenly lurched straight up, fifty feet into the air. As Alex stabbed at its controls, it jerked back and forth. It dived straight for the bottom of the steps. GOR-DON screamed as he waddled out of the way. His big, blobby belly hit the plaza just as the AirCar swooped, missing his shiny, newly bald head by an inch. Alex skidded the car up the museum steps and smashed through the giant entrance doors. They crashed to a halt in the lobby.

GO !!!

Chicago ran to the SquadCar and opened the door. Alex and Herbert were a bit dazed, but unharmed. "That was *awesome!*" Chicago said as they stumbled out of the car. He jumped behind the wheel. "Go!" he said. "I'll slow down the crowd!" He smiled at them. "And I thought this town was boring!"

Alex and Herbert watched as Chicago spun the SquadCar around and rammed it out the giant doorway. The SquadCar scraped back down the stairs and sent the approaching G'Dalien mob diving for cover again. Alex laughed, until his suit hit him in the head. He looked over at Herbert. "Let's go," said Herbert.

They ran toward the Hall of Human History.

The mob of G'Daliens surrounded the SquadCar. "We just want to talk!" one of them yelled, knocking politely on the window. "I'm sure this is all a big misunderstanding!" hollered another.

"Out of my way, you simps!" GOR-DON snarled
as he pushed the polite mob out of his way.
Mr. Illinois followed behind him and opened
the batwing door. Chicago smiled up at them.
GOR-DON grabbed Chicago by his shirt and
yanked him out of the squad car.

Mr. Illinois stepped up and stared sternly into GOR-DON's beady black eyes. "You take your suction cups off my son or I'll turn you into space-sushi, you read me?"

GOR-DON looked as if he might tear the detective's head off. Then he noticed the crowd, who were all staring at him. GOR-DON suddenly hugged Chicago, and gently set him down. "I'm so relieved," the lying G'Dalien blubbered. "Those two alien slayers haven't brainwashed you—yet."

"Dad," Chicago said. "They're not alien slayers. They're my friends."

Mr. Illinois looked at the crowd, then back at Chicago. "Sorry, son," he said. "This is my job. Which way did your friends go?"

Alex and Herbert rounded the corner and bounced off something warm and slimy.

"G'day, boys!" CA-ROL smiled as Alex and

Herbert scrambled to their feet. "My apologies for the inconvenience, but this exhibit is temporarily closed!"

Herbert thought fast. "How about the gift shop, CA-ROL?"

The helpful G'Dalien beamed. "*Terrif!*" she said, "I'll escort you myself!" She began leading them toward the lobby, pointing her tentacles at various items of interest. Alex and Herbert took one step, stopped as she turned the corner, and ran the other way.

They sped along the long Hallway of Human History, back toward the caveman diorama, frantically trying to put on and zip up their silver suits as they ran. The second time Alex tripped and fell on his face, Herbert signaled for him to stay down.

"Someone's coming!"

GOR-DON's shrieking voice echoed off the

massive museum walls.

"There's nowhere to hide!"
Herbert helped Alex to his
feet. The sound of tentacles
slapping against the smooth
floor grew louder. If they
continued down the hall, they'd be seen.

Alex glanced around and got an idea.

"Herbert, we have a solution," he said.

GOR-DON oozed into the center of the Hallway of Human History. *"There's no way out of this hallway, except through me,"* he sneered.

Chicago and his father were following him. "We're getting close," said Mr. Illinois.

Mr. Illinois glanced at Chicago and approached GOR-DON. "Look, I think you might be overreacting. I know these boys—"

"Silence, *Human!*" GOR-DON spat back, snorting through his fleshy nose holes. "They're close. I can smell their *fear.*" Chicago nervously glanced around, stopping at the diorama in front of them:

1969: G'DALIENS HELP EARTH-LINGS LOCATE THEIR MOON.

Chicago looked up at the four astronaut mannequins standing on the fake lunar surface. This was strange, because he'd learned in SchoolBooth that there'd been only two. Also

odd was the fact that the two short astronaut
mannequins wore helmets far too big for their
heads. They looked more like spaceman bobblehead
dolls. And one of the bobblehead spacemen was
having a very hard time standing still. "Oh, no,"
Chicago whispered to himself. Thinking quickly,
he pointed down the hall in the other direction and
hollered, "Hey! There they go!"

Chicago ran off, away from the bobblehead
astronauts. He didn't look back, but hoped that
his father and GOR-DON would follow him.

It almost worked. Mr. Illinois ran after his son, but GOR-DON had oozed only a few feet down the hallway when he heard a *CLUNK!* He spun around to see Alex toss his oversized space helmet over his shoulder alongside Herbert's as they both ran the other way.

"One small step for a man!" Herbert yelled back at GOR-DON.

"One giant leap away from you!" Alex added.

GOR-DON let out an angry growl and chased after them. He watched them as they jumped the railing of the very first diorama, near the beginning of the hallway.

G'DAY, PLEASE PARDON OUR MESS

He laughed. *"Nowhere to hide in there,"* he hissed.

Alex and Herbert leaped over the toppled cavemen. They hit their belt buckles as they approached the fake cave. Herbert's N.E.D. suit lit up. Alex's didn't.

Herbert, about to dive into the shimmering wormhole entrance, turned back and looked at Alex. "This is for your own good," he said.

He kicked Alex square in the belt buckle. Alex doubled over, but his suit whirred to life. The two of them frantically dived into the shimmering matter and disappeared into the painted-on cave entrance.

GOR-DON squeaked to a slimy stop in front of the prehistoric diorama—just as the wormhole closed, leaving only a wisp of blue smoke rising from the rock. His shiny black eyes scanned the scene but found only a pile of mannequin cavemen and a very relaxed-looking woolly mammoth staring at him. He entered the diorama and began overturning rocks, tossing cavemen, and pushing over trees. "Come out now, and I promise to kill you quickly," he

said, brushing aside a fake rock with a swat of
his tentacle. "Then I'll hold up *your* heads, this
time in front of City Hall, as examples of what a
dangerous species humans are. I'll have control
of this planet, and your kind as my slaves, by the
end of the week!"

He knocked the mammoth into another tree,
growing more angry by the minute. *"Now where
are you?!"* He kicked the headless caveman into

the fire and looked around at the diorama. It was completely trashed—and the humans were nowhere in sight. He grabbed a nearby caveman and tore its head off. Hurling it into the hallway, he screeched in frustration.

AAAAAAAAIIIEEEEEAA

20

Alex and Herbert flew out of the tunnel-slide and hit the soft grass of Alex's backyard. They looked at each other a moment and burst into wide grins. *"Totally awesome!"* Alex said.

WHAT ARE YOU GUYS, FOUR?

"Absolutely unprecedented!" Herbert agreed.

Sammi Clementine stood there, looking down.

"It's a *slide*. What could be so fun?" She waited for an answer, then marched over to the ladder. "Fine. Don't answer me. I'll see for myself."

Alex and Herbert jumped up.

"Do *not* do that," Herbert ordered.

"He's right," Alex said, "It's way too dangerous for you."

She looked down at them from the ladder. "Why? Because I'm a *girl? Please.* I'm a black belt in karate, a level four bungee jumper, and have a shaman's degree in snake-handling. I think I can survive your jungle gym." She pushed off, disappearing into the gaping mouth of the slide.

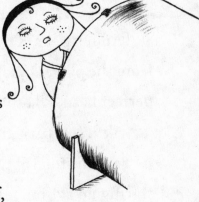

NOoo!!!

In an instant, Alex was at the top of the ladder, peering into the dark tube. "She did it!" he said. "Who knows what that slimy freak will do to her! I'm going back. I've got to save her."

"Uh, Alex," Herbert said.

"Don't try to stop me!" Alex yelled. "I'll face whatever that thing throws at me to get her back."

"Alex—"

"And I swear, if that six-legged alien-janitor from the planet Lysol lays one tentacle on her perfect head, I'll—"

"*Alex!*" He turned and looked down.

Sammi stood at the bottom of the slide, staring up at him. "You guys are so weird," she said, then ran to the fence, scaled it, and disappeared into her yard.

Herbert unzipped his silver N.E.D. suit. "Well, that was . . . *informative*," he said. "By which I mean, she saved us the trouble and risk of testing the slide, proving conclusively that wormhole-passage is impossible without my N.E.D. suits."

"She's not a guinea pig," Alex said.

"I know that," Herbert said. "A guinea pig's comparative biomass would be completely inadequate. That girl made the perfect test dummy."

Alex's suit hit Herbert in the head. "Y'know something? You can be a real jerk sometimes."

"*Me?!*" Herbert shot back. "You're the one who's made it too dangerous for us to return to the future!"

"What are you talking about?" Alex said.
"We're returning tomorrow! We promised
Chicago we'd play in his game. And a promise is
a—" Alex stopped himself.

"Are you insane?" Herbert said. "Forget
the game! An entire population of advanced
extraterrestrial beings thinks we're alien slayers,
all thanks to you and your stupid T-shirt—which
I assume you got from one of your stupid video
games!"

Alex stared at him and stepped forward
slowly. "Don't you use your fancy-pants sciencey
words on me. *What's a video game?*"

"Never mind," Herbert said. "I'm sure you'll figure it out soon enough."

"I'll go without you," Alex said. "It's *my* jungle gym."

"Great! Just be sure to wear your favorite *I ♥ TRAVELING THROUGH TIME* T-shirt," Herbert shot back, "because you won't be wearing *my* Negative Energy Density suit!"

Alex watched Herbert storm toward his house with the N.E.D.

suits. Then he plopped down on the grass and stared up at the blue tube. He knew Herbert was right. Without those suits, it was just a stupid slide.

"Y'know, I only wanted to see what you guys were playing."

Alex looked up. Sammi was leaning over the top of her fence.

"If you didn't want me to be part of your stupid

spaceman game, you could've just said so."

Alex got up and approached the fence. A weird feeling crept through his belly as he heard himself ask, "What are you doing tomorrow?"

She thought for a moment. "Tomorrow's Friday. I've got Crouching Ladybug Kung Fu in the morning, then hang-gliding lessons from eleven to one. Fifteen minutes for lunch, then extreme soapmaking."

"*Jeez*," Alex said. "Don't you get sick of having every minute of your summer planned out and scheduled for you?"

Sammi shrugged, then offered, "I'm on a waiting list for a Mommy & Me class on unstructured fun."

Alex stared at her. She looked down. He swallowed and said, "You want some unstructured fun? Meet me here, at the jungle gym, first thing tomorrow morning."

CHAPTER 21

The morning sunlight
crept through Herbert's
bedroom window,
followed by
a pink ninja and a kid
wearing red pajamas
and a Mexican wrestling mask. Sammi didn't
know why she was helping her strange neighbor
sneak into a strange bedroom to steal a pair
of silver suits, but already she knew that this
was the most fun she'd had all summer. What

Alex knew was that this already seemed too easy. He was sure that Herbert—who was snoring loudly with a thick book called *A Genius's Guide to Black Holes and Time Warps* lying across his face—would've hidden the N.E.D. suits before he went to sleep. But there they were, carelessly tossed on top of his laundry basket at the foot of his bed. He didn't even throw a dirty towel over them or think to get rid of the four red balloons tied to the basket, which made them ridiculously easy to find in his cluttered bedroom.

Alex pointed
at the suits,
and Sammi
nodded. She
noiselessly
did a double-
cartwheel
across the room, then gracefully dived
into a somersault, avoiding dozens of
half-built inventions and spare parts
that would've clattered Herbert out
of his slumber if she'd knocked into
them. Popping up in front of the laundry basket,
she snatched the suits from atop the dirty pile
of clothes. Again Alex thought, *This was way
too easy.* Then, as he noticed the balloons lifting
the laundry basket off the floor, he thought, *Or
maybe not.*

The basket reached the ceiling, where four

thumbtacks were glued, pointy-
sides down. The balloons
popped, startling Sammi and setting
off a complicated chain reaction
that ended with a bar
blocking Herbert's bedroom
door from the
outside, and a
beaker of acid
being splashed
onto a rope suspended from
the ceiling. Herbert yelled,
"Stop! Thieves!" He grabbed his
heavy book and hurled it just as the burned
rope snapped. Sammi spun into a leaping
roundhouse kick and deflected the book across
the room into the open window, wedging open a
door that was falling to block it. She tossed Alex
the suits and dove through the tight space held

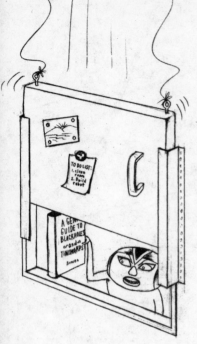

open by the book.

Alex climbed out behind her, but stopped to look back at Herbert, who was running toward him. "Mind if I borrow this?" he asked, putting a hand on the book. "I'm traveling today, and I could use a light read." Alex yanked the book and released the metal shield just as Herbert reached the window, sealing him inside his own room.

Sammi and Alex scrambled down the ivy beneath Herbert's bedroom window, jumped the fence, and reached the jungle gym.

Herbert bolted out his front door and ran over to Alex's house. As he approached, he saw Alex and Sammi climbing the top of the tunnel-slide and the shimmering blue light of the wormhole

reflecting off their silver suits. He reached the
ladder and climbed to the top just as Alex and
Sammi disappeared into the slide. Herbert closed
his eyes and dove in behind them. He felt a
powerful rush of air, heard an echoing *FOOMP!*—
and tasted a bitter taste in his mouth.

Herbert opened his eyes. He was lying on
the ground at the bottom of the slide in Alex's
backyard. He opened his mouth and spat out a
clump of grass and yelled.

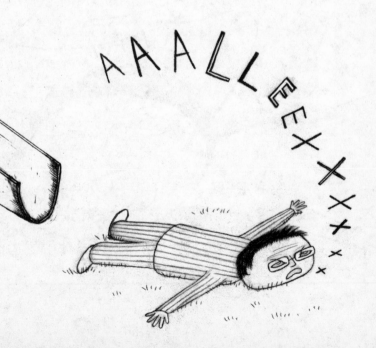

AAALLEEXXXXX

CHAPTER 23

GOR-DON stepped back to peer at his hard work. The trashed prehistoric diorama was now completely restored. The cavemen all had their heads again. The woolly mammoth stood at attention, her woolly fur shampooed and dried, her tusks scrubbed and polished. And most important, the G'Dalien UFO, saving the stupid human race yet again, was shined and waxed. Although GOR-DON hated humans, he took pride in his work—mostly because it told the story of how useless and doomed humans would be

without his species. This pleased him.

A floating MonitOrb drifted up the hallway,
reminding him what had caused
all of this destruction. It
projected the picture of Herbert
and Alex atop the SquadCar. At
the top of the video wanted poster
it said, *HAVE YOU SEEN US?*
GOR-DON snorted at the
weakhearted efforts by Inspector

Illinois to find the guilty humans, then he
spotted a smudge on the floor. GOR-DON
thought of smudges the same way he thought
of humans—he hated them both and lived for
wiping them all out. He oozed down the hall to
get his mop.

POP!

POP!

Alex and Sammi flew out of the fake cave and
slammed into the side of the woolly mammoth.

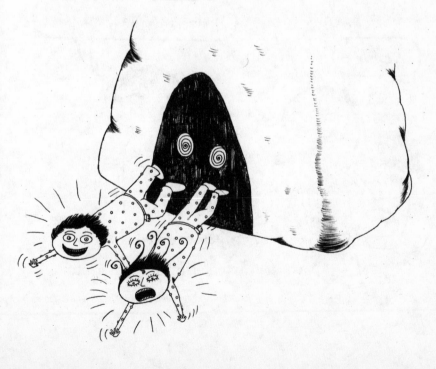

The newly cleaned stuffed beast teetered a bit, then slowly tipped over. Its long tusks snagged the edge of the fake G'Dalien UFO, yanking it down from the ceiling. The two biggest objects in the diorama hit the ground with a crash, knocking over the cavemen like bowling pins. Sammi stared at the mammoth in horror, as Alex snapped her out of it. "It's not real. C'mon, we've gotta stash these suits!" He helped her over the

WOW.

THAT WAS NOTHING.

railing and quickly led her down the hallway.

GOR-DON came back around the corner with his mop, glanced up at the diorama, then dunked his mop into his bucket. He froze, and slowly looked up again. Staring at the trashed scene, his jaggedy-toothed mouth fell open.

From somewhere deep within his alien throat emerged a small gurgling sound.

Alex led Sammi on a tour through the streets of Merwinsville. He was acting as if he'd built it all himself. "See that over there?" he said. "That's the Memory Bank. I have so many memories in there. Seriously. I really do." Sammi was half listening, trying to take it all in as Alex pointed to the huge golf-tee building. "And that there's City Hall. It's see-through and run by G'Daliens." She stared up at it, but a huge MonitOrb floating up above caught her eye.

"Wow, you really know this town," she said.

Alex smiled, "Well, I guess you could say it's like home to me."

"And they really seem to know you." She gestured toward the MonitOrb screen. They both stopped and stared up at Alex and Herbert's digital wanted poster.

"So are you guys in some kind of trouble?"

Sammi asked.

Alex glanced around. There were MonitOrbs everywhere, showing the same image. He looked up. Their faces were being blasted across huge screens all over the city. He glanced across the street and thought he saw two G'Daliens whispering as they looked right at him. Panicking, he grabbed her hand and pulled her over to a corner street pole, where he shoved his head into a hair-helmet. It beeped, and Alex pulled his head out. Sammi laughed. Hard.

"Hey, great disguise!" Alex heard a familiar voice. "Nobody'll ever recognize you guys dressed in regular clothes." Chicago turned to Sammi. "And *Herbalulu!* If I didn't know this was a costume, I'd ask you out on a date!"

Sammi looked at Alex.

"Uh, Chicago—," said Alex, "Herbalulu kinda

overslept today. This is, uh, Sammi . . . *land*."

Chicago's face turned almost as red as Sammi's. "Sorry," Chicago said. "I guess I thought—"

"It's okay," Sammi beamed. "Nice to meet you."

Something about the way Sammi was smiling at Chicago bugged Alex, and he was happy to change the subject. "Hey, sorry about yesterday," he said. "You really helped us. I hope we didn't get you in any trouble."

"Are you kidding? That was the most fun I've had in a long time! Forget it," Chicago said. "Besides, we've got a game to concentrate on now."

CHAPTER

24

Alex's mom found Herbert sitting in the backyard, glaring angrily at the bottom of the slide. Alex's little sister, Ellie, sat beside him, as did her teddy bear, Mr. Snugglebuns. All three were wearing pajamas.

"Hi, Mommy. Herbert is sad," she said. "So Mr. Snugglebuns and I are throwing him a daytime pajama party."

"That's great, sweetie," she said, turning her

attention to Herbert. "Herbie? Are you all right?"

"I'm perfectly fine, Mrs. Filby," Herbert said, sounding not fine at all.

"Where's Alex?" she asked. "He said he'd be playing at your house today. You two are still best friends, I hope."

"Oh, *yes*. In fact, my *best friend* woke me up bright and early today. Couldn't wait to get started. *What a pal!*"

Mrs. Filby looked relieved. "Oh, good. Because I got something for both of you. To share. Together."

Mrs. Filby pulled a familiar-looking box out of a bag.

"The gentleman at the video game store told me it's the last one in the entire western hemisphere," she said. "I had to bodycheck three teenagers to get my hands on it." She chuckled. "We told Alex no more video games this summer, but an article in *Perfect Parenting* magazine said playing these games can improve neurological dexterity, which sounded to me like something he might need."

Mrs. Filby handed Herbert a brand-new AlienSlayer: 3-D! video game system, complete with motion-synchronized weapons and, most importantly to Herbert, two brand-new *motion-sensor bodysuits*. "Would you mind giving it to Alex when you see him?" she asked.

"Oh, don't worry, Mrs. Filby," Herbert grinned. "I'll see that he gets it."

Herbert tore back to his room, locked the door and wrote his primary objectives on his chalkboard, "to-do" list-style.

He'd finished his first objective by lunchtime.

- ☑ Modify AS:3-D! Bodysuit.
- ☐ Figure out a way to transport AS:3-D! game to future.
- ☐ Travel to future.
- ☐ Find Ignoramus Maximus (a.k.a. Alex).
- ☐ Smash AS:3-D! game to bits in front of him. Laugh in his face as he cries like a baby. (Get picture, if possible.)

The second one would be a bit trickier. According to everything he'd read on multi-dimensional wormhole theory (which was a lot), attempting to pass electronic devices through a wormhole could have extremely dangerous results. Luckily, he had a brilliant idea. *Again.*

Herbert wheeled his solar-powered Red Rider
wagon up to Andretti's Pizzeria, careful not to
park it in the shade. He pulled out an old, plastic
suitcase and spun its built-in combination lock.
"Three . . . Fourteen . . . Eighteen . . . Seventy-nine."

CLICK!

Herbert opened the suitcase and checked it

carefully. Set snugly inside was the AS:3-D! game. He closed it and spun the dial numbers to set the lock. Then he glanced around to make sure no one was watching. He looked down the street leading up to Andretti's and saw normal cars, normal buildings, and normal sidewalks—ones without huge, squidlike creatures oozing up and down them. *All of this will be gone in the next century*, he thought. *All of it except . . .*

He turned and smiled up at good ol' Andretti's Pizzeria. With the suitcase tucked under his arm, he snuck around the side alley and climbed a fire escape ladder. Once on the roof, he looked around. He ran to the stairwell door in the center of the roof. Beside it was a large air-conditioning vent. He took one last look around to make sure he was alone, and then stashed the suitcase containing the AS:3-D! game just inside the vent where no one—but he—would ever find it.

CHAPTER 25

Sammi stared down at the city drifting below her. "And I thought there was a lot to do in Merwinsville *before*," she said. Her voice sounded funny because she had her nose pressed against the window of the Anti-GraviTram. Alex kept his head turned toward the window, too. But he was trying to hide his face from the passengers on the tram. Every few minutes a floating MonitOrb would pass by outside, mega-projecting his face next to Herbert's along with the words *HAVE YOU SEEN US?* He was just waiting for a G'Dalien commuter to jump up, yank off his giant curly hairdo and yell, *"Aha!!"*

Chicago leaned over to Alex and whispered, "Don't worry. Even if they recognized you, they wouldn't care—everyone's headed to today's big Meteors game."

Alex sneaked a peek. It was true. Nearly everyone on the tram, humans and G'Daliens alike, had hats or T-shirts or little flags. And they all said, *GO, METEORS!!*, or something similar.

"Besides," Chicago continued, "even my dad doesn't believe that crazy janitor. And he'd really like to. It'd make his job a lot more interesting."

"So what's with the wanted signs all over the city?"

Chicago shrugged. "Dad had his department put those out. He'll give you guys an I-DNA scan, verify you on the Global

HAVE YOU SEEN US?

Directory, and let you go. Then he can file a case report. Poor guy never gets to file case reports."

Alex had no idea what an I-DNA scan was, or a Global Directory, but they both sounded like things he should probably avoid. "So, uh, where's your dad now?" he asked carefully.

"That nutty G'Dalien called him up to the museum again," Chicago said. "Now he can't coach us tonight!" Alex felt relieved that he wouldn't be seeing Chicago's dad. This feeling lasted exactly two and a half seconds.

"Whoa!" Sammi said from the window. "Is *that* where you guys are playing?!"

Alex stepped over to the window. Below was a gigantic, perfectly white boulder, the size of a football stadium. Alex laughed.

The entire tram, humans and G'Daliens alike, suddenly jumped up and broke into a cheer. They began patting Chicago on the back.

"Wait a minute," Alex said nervously. "Who are the Meteors, exactly?"

Chicago plopped a METEORS baseball cap on top of Alex's massive, shrublike hairdo. "*We are!*" he said. The fans cheered again, this time breaking out into a horrible song about the Meteors.

The tram doors opened and they were flushed out along with the singing fans. Alex saw thousands more streaming into the giant rock-shaped arena. He had a strong urge to run and hide.

Before he could, Sammi grabbed his arm. "This is so *cool!*" she whispered. "Thank you for bringing me here!"

Alex forced a smile, turned, and followed Chicago toward a marked door—*ATHLETES ONLY.*

CHAPTER 26

CHAPTER
27

POP! Herbert hit the rocky dirt in front of the fake cave. He quickly switched off his suit, hopped the railing, and turned down the Hallway of Human History.

GOR-DON stood there wearing an evil grin on his puffy face and a boo-boo bandage on his upper lip. Beside him was Mr. Illinois. LO-PEZ stood in the back, eating from a bag of muffins.

GOR-DON stepped closer to Herbert. He held in his tentacles Alex and Sammi's silver N.E.D. suits. "Oh, *goody*," he snarled. "Another *Alien-*

Slayer Army uniform. I'll add it to my collection."

"There's no army," Herbert said. "It's just my two friends. And none of us are alien slayers— they only came to play in some stupid T-ball game!"

Mr. Illinois and LO-PEZ shared a sudden look of concern.

GOR-DON gasped. *"Did you hear him?!"* he hissed. "The whole city's trapped in that stadium with those killers! What are we waiting for?"

"I'm in charge here, Gordo," Mr. Illinois said. "Why don't you just back on down."

"It's GOR-DON."

Mr. Illinois pulled out his detective's notebook and took a step toward Herbert. "Now, I know you'd never lie to me, *Herbalulu*. And I want to believe you and your friend. But some new evidence has come to light, and it doesn't look good. Especially for your friend."

Mr. Illinois flipped open the notepad. A small lens popped up. GOR-DON handed the detective his small green cube. Mr. Illinois

DIE! DIE! DIE!!

snapped it into his notepad. Suddenly projected in thin air above them, as big as a movie theater screen, was Alex's memory of playing video games.

Mr. Illinois was right. It didn't look good. Not at all. Alex was standing in his bedroom, holding a blaster in his hand, yelling, *"You want summa that, you bug-eyed slimebags? Come and get it, slug-monkeys!! Die! Die! Die!!"* He was playing AlienSlayer 2, and boy was he slaying aliens. A *lot* of aliens. Herbert watched Alex happily blast them into tiny bits of green goo. He saw how this might look pretty disturbing if you didn't realize it was just a video game—and if you happened to be an alien.

"Turn it off!" GOR-DON suddenly fake-sobbed, "I can't bear to watch! Oh, the horror! *The horror!*" Mr. Illinois handed him the green cube and GOR-DON stopped crying immediately.

Mr. Illinois suddenly looked very serious— more so than usual. "Son, just tell me who you are and where you're from, and we can put this whole thing behind us."

Herbert thought a moment. "Sorry, sir, but I can't," he said. "And you'd never believe me, even if I could."

GOR-DON snorted.

"Then you leave me no choice." Mr. Illinois snapped his fingers. LO-PEZ stuffed four muffins into his mouth in order to free up a tentacle to hand his boss a small device. It was marked *I-DNA SCANNER.* "This won't hurt a bit," Mr. Illinois said. He pressed the I-DNA Scanner to Herbert's arm. Herbert felt a warm pulse shoot through his body. The device beeped.

"There," Mr. Illinois said. "We'll locate your identity on the Global Directory, and I can file my case repor—" He stopped mid-sentence.

"What's it say?" GOR-DON blurted. "*Who is he?*"

Mr. Illinois glanced at his partner. A chunk of muffin fell out of LO-PEZ's mouth.

"*Who IS he?!*" The veins in
GOR-DON's spongy
head-flesh were now
throbbing.

"The I-DNA scan says he's
Herbert Slewg," Mr. Illinois
said. "Born and raised right
here in Merwinsville."

Herbert's face brightened.

"Right! That's me!"

"Look son, I don't know how you
fooled the scanner, but you *can't*
be Herbert Slewg," Mr. Illinois
said. "According to the Global
Directory,
Herbert Slewg
is *one hundred
and ten years old.*"

CHAPTER 28

Alex walked out of the Meteors' locker room, through the dugout, and onto the field. "Oh, no," he said. Endless rows of seats were built into the craggy walls of the Meteor-Dome, and they were filled with human and G'Dalien fans. The Meteors fans

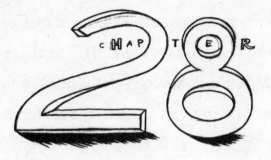

munched on Meteor-Dogs, sipped bright green liquid from humongous rock-shaped drink cups, sang terrible songs terribly, and cheered at highlights from past A.G. T-Ball games shown on a huge MonitOrb floating in the center of the dome.

Dallas slapped Alex on the back, a bit too hard. "See?" he said thickly. "This guy's *funny!*"

EL-ROY was also scanning the crowd. "Actually, there are still two seats left, so technically today's match isn't even sold out."

"*Sold out?*" Alex snapped. "We're ten years old! Who'd pay to see a bunch of little kids play an even *littler kid's* recess game? There isn't even a *pitcher!*"

The team stopped strapping thick, heavy pads to their bodies and stared at him. Sausalito tucked his long hair into his helmet and burst out in a high-pitched laugh. The rest of them busted up along with him.

Alex felt dizzy. He sat down at the end of the bench. Sammi sat down beside him. "Hey, did I tell you how, last summer, at CowKids Rodeo Camp, I won the age seven-to-nine Bull-riding Finals?"

"Wow. That's awesome for you," Alex said, frozen in terror.

"It was actually pretty scary. I had to compete in front of a huge crowd of whoopin', hollerin', real-live cowboys—not to mention my parents. Wanna know how I did it?" Alex looked at her. She grinned and jumped up. "Glad you asked!"

She picked up an A.G. T-ball helmet and shoved it onto his head. It pushed his poofy hairdo out the sides, and the rim almost covered his eyes.

"Ow!" he said. "What'd you do, *annoy* the bulls into letting you ride them?"

"Shut up and *look*," she said. "Out there."

Alex looked. With the helmet pulled tight, he couldn't see the giant MonitOrb or the crowd jammed into the stands above him. With the hair jutting out over his ears, he couldn't see the crowd on either side, and their loud cheers were muffled. All he saw was what was directly in front of him—*a T-ball field*. He slowly stood up.

It was a baseball diamond, with three oversized bases and a little plastic tee standing waist-high at home plate. Balanced on top of the tee was a ball, just sitting there, waiting to be hit.

"Did I mention I broke the bull-riding camp record?" Sammi said. "Broke my collarbone, too, but it was *totally* worth it."

Alex stared out at the field. He felt better immediately. "You're right." He laughed. "It's just *T-ball!* My little sister Ellie could play this!"

WHUMP! A big pile of equipment hit the bench.

"Better get suited up," Chicago said. "Almost game time." Alex looked down at the thick pads. Sammi picked up the glove and followed Chicago.

"Are you guys still short a player?"

Chicago nodded. Sammi smiled and held a glove to her hip.

"Oh, right. Funny." He turned away.

The thick baseball glove tagged him in the back of the head, and he spun back around.

"Strike *one*," Sammi

said, glaring at him and holding a helmet threateningly.

"I didn't make the No Girls Allowed rule! Go throw stuff at the A.G. T-Ball Commission!"

Sammi scoffed. "What's 'A.G' stand for, *All Guys?*"

Chicago gave her a look. Finally he said, "You should probably sit down—and buckle up." Sammi looked down at the bench. There were seat belts bolted to it.

"LADIES AND GENTLEMEN, HUMANS AND G'DALIENS!" The faces of two announcers—one from each species—looked down from the MonitOrb. Their voices boomed throughout the stadium. *"TIME TO LOCK AND LOAD!"*

Sammi looked at the crowd. Padded shoulder-bars extended from each seat, securing each fan in his or her seat. The fans grew more excited, and they chimed in with the announcers: *"LET'S*

PLAAAY ANTI-GRAVI-TEEEE-BALLLLL!!"

A stage drifted out onto center field, carrying a giant light switch and a group of girls in matching hats and uniforms, waving to the crowd. "*HERE TO FLIP THE CEREMONIAL GRAVITY KILL-SWITCH IS LOCAL STARSCOUT TROOP 76! READY GIRLS? THREE . . . TWO . . . ONE . . . FLIP IT!!*" The StarScout Girls displayed impressive teamwork as they attacked the giant switch and pulled it to the *OFF* position.

The stadium jolted. It began to hum. The crowd, secured by their shoulder-bars, rose an inch off their seats.

The StarScout Girls, strapped to the float, drifted above the field and dangled like a bunch of Scout-shaped party balloons. Similarly, the three oversized bases were released and drifted straight up, over the infield. Tethered to the ground by twenty-five-foot chains, the hovering bases strained to break free.

Sammi looked down. She was two feet off the ground, and rising. "I told you to buckle up!" Chicago said, tossing her a thick chest pad. The heavy gear brought her back down. She looked over and saw the rest of the team bouncing and bobbing comfortably and in control, weighted down by their heavy equipment. She looked for Alex, but didn't see him.

"Hey! Up here!" Alex was six feet above the

bench, dangling in the air with only one pad half strapped on. Sammi scrambled over and pulled him back down.

"C'mon, Alexville!" Chicago moon-bounced over to the two of them. "Quit goofing around—you're up first!"

Herbert was crammed beside GOR-DON in the back of the SquadCar as they zipped toward the Meteor-Dome. He flattened himself as far as he could against his door in an attempt to create some distance between his body and GOR-DON's. The conniving alien had taken his N.E.D. suit, which meant that in the gym shorts and button-down short-sleeved shirt he had on underneath, Herbert's bare arms and legs were sticking to GOR-DON's gooey flesh. It felt like a giant rubber glove filled with warmed-up snot.

"Psst." The creature leaned in closer. *"Just wanted to thank you for helping me take over the world,"* he whispered.

"Soon I will convince every G'Dalien in that stadium, then in this city, and finally on this planet—that the human race is a species to be feared and exterminated, rather than trusted and helped. The moronic masses will honor and venerate me so greatly that they will make me their leader—and Marion will see me rule this pathetic lump you once called Earth."

"Who's *Marion?*" Herbert asked.

"What?"

"You said, '*Marion.*'"

"No I didn't."

"You did. You said, '*Marion* will see me rule this pathetic lump, etcetera, etceter—'"

"I did not say 'Marion'!"

Herbert shrugged and turned to look out the

window. He couldn't fear too much for either his life or the Earth's future because each time he spotted a MonitOrb zoom past with his and

Alex's giant faces below the words *HAVE YOU SEEN US?*, he could only feel anger.

This was all because of Alex. Specifically, because of Alex's idiotic love of those idiotic video games. *That's the common variable to this whole mess,* Herbert thought. First, Alex's dumb T-shirt. Then, Alex's incriminating memory of playing AlienSlayer 2. And finally, his total obsession with AlienSlayer: 3-D!, which made Herbert think to hide it on the roof of Andretti's for a hundred years, just so he could come to the future, find Alex, and smash it in front of him.

Herbert smiled a little at this last notion. That

would have been very satisfying, he thought. Alex
would've felt what it was like to see something
he loved get taken away. His cherished game
would've been destroyed, along with its stupid
built-in holographic projection unit making
the game look, feel, and sound like the invading
aliens were real and in the room with you—

Herbert stopped. The thoughts racing
through his brain suddenly slammed into
the sights flashing past his eyeballs. At that
moment, he happened to look down and spot the
unmistakably twenty-first-century-style roof of
Andretti's Pizzeria. This triggered an ingenious
idea. *Again.* In a split second, Herbert realized
how to save Alex and Sammi, get the N.E.D. suits
back, stop GOR-DON's evil plan to take over the
world, and fix everything.

But first he had to get LO-PEZ to stop for
lunch.

"Hey, you guys," he suddenly blurted out. "Who's hungry?"

GOR-DON glared at him.

Mr. Illinois didn't respond. But LO-PEZ, who hadn't had anything to eat for fifteen minutes, turned his head ever so slightly, which was all Herbert needed.

HEY, WHO'S HUNGRY?

"Man," Herbert continued, staring at LO-PEZ. "I could sure go for a nice, thick, cheesy, topping-filled slice of Andretti's pizz—"

Suddenly, Herbert's entire face was wrapped in warm, snot-like alien flesh. But he didn't mind. In fact, somewhere under the rolls of blobby flab, Herbert smiled. Because the fact that GOR-DON had suddenly been thrown on top of him was the direct result of LO-PEZ pulling a sudden midair U-turn. And that meant that step one of Herbert's ingenious plan was underway.

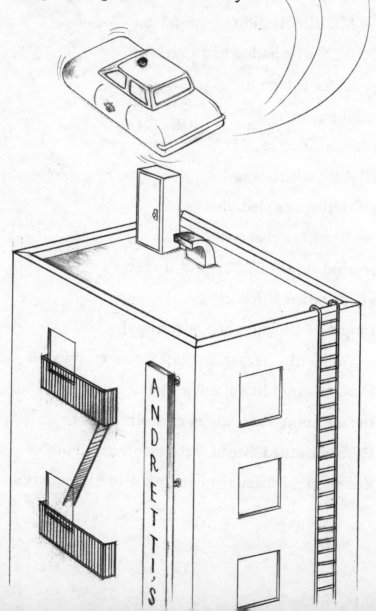

CHAPTER
30

The G'Dalien announcer's voice boomed from
the massive MonitOrb, echoing off the walls of
the Meteor-Dome. The crowd burst into a loud
roar as the Thrashers bounded out onto the field.
They were big, mean-looking, and clearly used
to playing without gravity. Alex stared in awe as
they flipped and leaped, bouncing off the walls,
the floating bases, even each other.

"BATTING FIRST FOR THE METEORS, NUMBER
THIRTEEN, ALEXVILLE!" Alex woke from his
daze, grabbed a bat, and awkwardly float-stepped

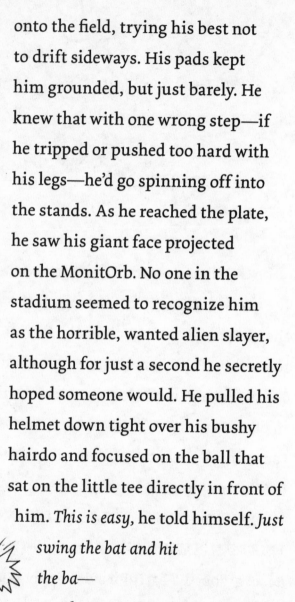

onto the field, trying his best not to drift sideways. His pads kept him grounded, but just barely. He knew that with one wrong step—if he tripped or pushed too hard with his legs—he'd go spinning off into the stands. As he reached the plate, he saw his giant face projected on the MonitOrb. No one in the stadium seemed to recognize him as the horrible, wanted alien slayer, although for just a second he secretly hoped someone would. He pulled his helmet down tight over his bushy hairdo and focused on the ball that sat on the little tee directly in front of him. *This is easy*, he told himself. *Just swing the bat and hit the ba—*

The tee suddenly blasted the

ball straight up into the air. The crowd erupted, and the Thrashers pushed off the ground and began to leap toward him. Alex panicked.

Chicago and the others were yelling for him to do something. He couldn't hear them over the crowd. They pointed up at the ball, fifty feet above his head. Sammi stretched her arms over her head, like Superman. Alex suddenly realized what they were all trying to tell him, and his stomach sank.

They want me to fly? he said to himself. Alex swallowed hard, crouched down, and shot himself straight up into the air. Right past the ball.

CLUNK—"*Oof!*" Alex slammed into the bottom of the floating MonitOrb. His helmet popped off and he floated up, up, and away. He looked down. "Oh, no!"

The Thrashers bounced toward the gently floating T-ball. And while this was clearly not his little sister's game, Alex was pretty sure that as the batter, he was supposed to get to the ball before the other team. He pushed off the MonitOrb and launched himself downward. As he approached the ball, he closed his eyes and swung.

CRACK! The crowd roared as the ball flew toward the outfield. "*Woooohoooo!*" Alex yelled—right up until he hit the ground.

He flattened the tee at home plate, but immediately jumped to his feet. Full of adrenaline, Alex began to run toward first base, or where first base would be if it weren't floating twenty-five feet above the ground. He took an over-enthusiastic step, however, and it sent him spinning up in the air. *"Aaaaahhhh!"* Alex yelled as he floated, upside down, above the first-base line.

Alex could only watch as his ball, helped along by zero gravity, zoomed high above the centerfielder's head, bounced off the ground, hit the back wall, and spun straight up into the air. The Thrashers' outfielder launched himself, twenty, thirty, forty feet into the air and snatched the ball. In one skillful move, he pivoted and threw it to the Thrashers' first

baseman—a beefy kid named Brockton, who was as big as he was mean.

"Haw haw!" Brockton laughed as he pushed off the

ground to catch the ball, careful not to tag Alex
out at first. Since Alex was still stuck spinning
his legs above the first-base line like a spider
trapped in a toilet bowl, this would've been
easy. *"Too easy!"* the thuggish Thrasher yelled
out. Instead, Brockton swung himself off the
stiff anchor-chain beneath the base and zoomed
straight for Alex, cleats-first. He slammed
Alex, sending him
tumbling into the
dirt in front of the
Meteors'
dugout. It
was cruel,
unnecessary,
and completely
within the rules
of A.G. T-Ball.
"Booooo!" yelled the angry crowd. Brockton

bounded across the field and into the arms of his laughing teammates as the human announcer's voice boomed, "Chain slam! *Heeee's out!*"

Dallas removed Alex's pads and effortlessly floated him over to the Meteors' dugout, where Sammi glared out at the high-fiving Thrashers. "C'mon, Alex," she said as she unbuckled herself. "I've got you." She turned and gave Brockton one more dose of stink eye as she floated Alex toward the locker room.

BO o

BO o

BO o

CHAPTER 31

"LO-PEZ!*"* Mr. Illinois barked. *"*We are in *hot pursuit* of a suspect or suspects—stopping for pizza is not proper protocol!*"* LO-PEZ opened his door and oozed out of the SquadCar, onto the roof of Andretti's Pizzeria.

The overweight alien looked at his boss. He counted with his tentacles: *"One,* we know who they are. *Two,* we know *where* they are. *Three,* they don't know *we know* who or where they are. *Four,* they aren't going anywhere. And most importantly, *five*—I haven't eaten in twenty minutes.*"*

In the backseat, GOR-DON's head-veins were throbbing again. "*You fat idiot!*" he yelled.

"Oh yeah, thanks for reminding me, mate." LO-PEZ said. He held up his last tentacle. "*Six—*" His last tentacle shot into the backseat and around GOR-DON's neck. "*I really don't like you!*" Mr. Illinois spun around and pulled LO-PEZ's tentacle off GOR-DON's bulging gullet.

GOR-DON made overdramatic choking noises as he caught his breath. "Are you going to let him get away with that?"

Mr. Illinois glanced at LO-PEZ, then turned back to the gasping G'Dalien in his backseat. *"Hey—Nobody talks to my partner that way but me, you got that, Gorgon?"*

"It's GOR-DON."

LO-PEZ shared a nod with Mr. Illinois, then turned toward the rooftop stairs. Herbert suddenly hopped out of the SquadCar and followed him. *"Hey!"* GOR-DON yelled, "The suspect is trying to escape! *Kill him!*" Mr. Illinois spun around again and faced the janitor alien. "My partner's escorting the suspect. Now I suggest you stick a mop in it, *Google*, before you start getting on my nerves."

"It's GOR-DON!!!"

LO-PEZ and Herbert approached the rooftop

stairwell of Andretti's. Herbert immediately spotted the air-conditioning vent. He knelt down in front of it. "Sorry," he said. "Leg fell asleep from being crammed in the backseat next to that slimeball."

LO-PEZ nodded. "Wanna know somethin'?" he said. "There's something shonky about that guy. I don't care what proof he's got, I ain't buying it. If you kids are alien-slaying bushrangers, I'm a vegetarian. And I'm not."

Herbert grinned. "Then you can help me!" He reached into the vent, felt around with his hands, and pulled out the plastic suitcase. It was stained and covered with cobwebs, but right where he'd left it a hundred years ago. Herbert immediately noticed something odd. He read the combination on the suitcase. *His* combination.

"Three . . . Fourteen . . . Eighteen . . . Seventy-nine . . ." Herbert lifted the latch. The suitcase had been opened—and emptied. The AlienSlayer:3-D! game was gone. "Impossible!" he said.

"Fair dinkums," LO-PEZ said. "An old, moldy, empty suitcase, crammed into a vent. That *is* impossible. Well, pretty darned unlikely, anyway. Okay, time to eat." LO-PEZ turned and began to ooze down the stairs.

"But no one knew that combination but me!" Herbert dropped the suitcase and slumped behind LO-PEZ toward the wafting smell of cheese and tomato sauce. The AS:3-D! game had vanished, and so had his ingenious plan.

There were no customers. The G'Dalien waiter was watching the A.G. T-Ball game on a small MonitOrb floating above the empty bumper-car tables. He looked up as Herbert and LO-PEZ approached. "Hey! Why aren't you guys at the game? You shoulda seen it! This new player for the Meteors *stinks!* Got chain-slammed on the very first play their *first time up*, and now the Thrashers are up!"

Herbert slumped a little more. He didn't know what a *"chain-slam"* was, but he was pretty sure he knew the stinky player who got one.

CHAPTER 32

With Alex out of the game and recovering in the locker room, the Meteors were now short two players. EL-ROY had to cover the entire outfield. He wasn't a very fast runner, but he could wear six baseball gloves at the same time, which helped. Dallas was at third base, and Sausalito was covering first. That left Chicago in the middle of the infield, playing both second base and shortstop. This was the best they could do. They had no chance at stopping the Thrashers.

The floating, chain-tethered bases were loaded. Three Thrashers stood balancing atop first, second, and third, high above the field. And up next was their best hitter—Brockton. The crowd booed as the MonitOrb replayed in super-slow-motion the chain-slam he'd given Alex last inning.

From second base, Chicago watched with dread as Brockton approached the plate. He knew what was coming. Brockton soaked in the hatred of the crowd, smiling and waving to the booing mob.

Looking past home plate, Chicago noticed a player step out of the Meteors' dugout. He called a time-out and bounced across the infield, then burst into a wide grin when he saw the number 13 on the player's jersey. "Alexville!" He floated down to him and hugged him. "Alexville! You sure you're all right to play?" Number 13 wore a tint-masked helmet, but nodded. "Great!" Chicago said.

He pointed toward home plate. Brockton stood there, looking impatient. "That's the ape who chain-slammed you. He's a real longball-hitter, so I want you and EL-ROY to split the outfield. Get out there, Alexville, and let's see what you got!" The helmet nodded again, and Number 13 bounced off, reaching right field in just a few leaping bounds.

The ball shot out of the tee and flew straight up into the air. Brockton launched himself upward,

CRACK

soaring toward it. He
swung—*CRACK!* The *YEEEHAWWWW*
ball went screaming
into deep right field, straight for Number
13. Chicago watched it sail overhead
and yelled, *"Your ball, Alexville!"*

Instead of going for
the ball, Number 13
leaped away from it and
landed in front of
EL-ROY. *"Hey!"* EL-ROY squealed as he was picked
up like a sack of potatoes and thrown into the
air. Realizing he was headed straight for the ball,
he yelled, *"Awright! Goodonya, Alexville!"* The tiny
G'Dalien grabbed it in midair as it ricocheted off
the back wall, then fired it toward the Thrasher
running from third base to home.

What no one noticed as they watched
EL-ROY's spectacular play was that after

throwing his teammate, Number 13 had immediately bounded across the infield. He dived and intercepted EL-ROY's throw, tagging the surprised Thrasher out with a karate kick to the legs.

"ONE OUT!" The announcers shouted in unison.

Number 13 then triple-backflipped over to Dallas, who watched in amazement from the ground beneath third base. *"Go, Alexville!"* Dallas yelled as he caught his twirling teammate and launched him straight upward, just as the runner was about to leap from second base to third. He slammed directly into the Thrasher, and the two of them spun above the base, tangled in midair.

"TWO OUTS!" the announcers boomed.

Number 13 grabbed the Thrasher in a wrestling hold and spun him around as they began to descend toward the field. He flung the player directly into the runner who'd reached second. This wasn't an out, technically, but it *took* him out. He was knocked off second base by his flailing teammate, and the two of them tumbled into the outfield, where EL-ROY was enjoying the show.

"Good bit of base running there, mates!" he guffawed at them.

This left Brockton standing on first base with two outs and all his teammates cleared from the bases. Ordinarily he would've stayed put, but he noticed something in the outfield. His teammate, Philadelphia, who'd tangled with Number 13, was holding something up—*a weighted chest pad*. Philly had cheated—he'd stripped off Number 13's gear.

Brockton looked up. Alex was floating away. Within seconds he was too high above the field to be able to throw the ball down to his teammates. A few more seconds and he was sailing past the MonitOrb, straight for the craggy ceiling of the Meteor-Dome.

"*Yes!*" Brockton pumped his fist in the air as he bounded casually toward second base, watching Alex drift higher and higher. Rounding second, he waved to the fans who yelled, *"Cheater! Cheater!"* High above them all, Alex slammed into a stalactite at the top of the Meteor-Dome. Brockton bounced high over third, and gracefully stretched out his toe to tap it.

Then suddenly, the base dropped out of his reach.

The bases crashed to the

ground, as did the bouncing
fielders. Brockton also dropped
like a stone, hitting the dirt with
a dull thud.

The crowd fell back into their
seats. They gasped as Number 13, high above the
field, now clung helplessly from his stalactite.

Brockton's last few feet to home plate were
not easy. His heavy pads made it feel like he was
pulling a truck filled with refrigerators packed
with frozen turkeys, uphill. He heard the roar
of the crowd and looked
up. High above him, Alex
let go of the stalactite. He
stretched out his oversized
jersey with his arms and
launched himself, using
the wind resistance to soar
through the air like a flying

squirrel. Brockton screamed as he crawled toward the plate. Just a he got close, the ninja-squirrel zoomed in at an angle and slammed into the heavily padded Thrasher. The two of them tumbled to a stop down the baseline, kicking up a huge cloud of dust.

The stadium grew silent as the dust settled. Brockton was lying with arms and fingers outstretched, reaching for—but not quite touching—home plate. From underneath him, a baseball mitt slowly emerged. It lifted off the ground and the hand inside it opened slowly—the ball rolled out of the mitt and clunked Brockton on the head.

"HE'S OUT!" the announcers roared. "LADIES AND GENTLEMEN, YOU JUST WITNESSED THE FIRST SINGLE-PLAYER TRIPLE PLAY IN A.G. T-Ball HISTORY!"

The crowd went crazy. And with the gravity restored, they were free to leap to their feet without fear of injury or death.

"Way to go, Alexville!" Chicago pulled his teammate out from under the defeated Thrasher and hugged him tightly. The rest of the team lifted the two of them up onto their shoulders, cheering and high-fiving, and carried them to the dugout.

They suddenly stopped short.

Stepping onto the field in just his underpants, holding an icepack and eating a Meteor-Dog, *was Alex.*

"What's all the noise about?" he asked, looking up at Chicago. "And why are you *hugging her?*"

Chicago released the person in Alex's jersey and pulled off the tint-masked helmet. Sammi shook out her hair and smiled at him.

"How did you—?" he stammered.

Sammi shrugged. "Let's see. Black belt in

Jujitsu. Greco-Roman wrestling lessons since I was six. Acrobat Circus and Extreme Gymnastics sleepaway camp last year came in handy—oh, and Lassie League MVP, four summers in a row." She smiled at the stunned captain of the Meteors.

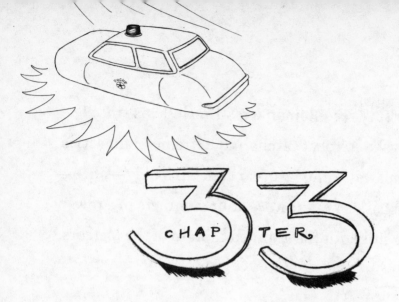

CHAPTER 33

Clouding the excitement from the mystery triple-playmaker was the question nearly everyone in the Meteor-Dome had on their minds: *Who turned on the gravity?* A loud, whirring sound from above soon provided an answer, as a circle in the center of the ceiling retracted. The *Human/G'Dalien Harmony Enforcement* SquadCar air-dropped in and hovered an inch above the center of the field. The batwing doors opened and LO-PEZ stepped out, munching on a slab of pizza.

Mr. Illinois got out next and flipped open his tricked-out detective's notebook. As he spoke into it, his voice boomed through the MonitOrb, across the entire stadium. *"ATTENTION CITIZENS! THERE IS NO NEED TO PANIC!"*

GOR-DON popped out of the car and shoved Mr. Illinois to one side, grabbing his megaphone-notebook. *"DO NOT LISTEN TO THIS HUMAN!"* he shrieked into it.

GOR-DON continued. "*THE HUMAN SITTING NEXT TO YOU IS NOT YOUR FRIEND! HE WISHES TO DESTROY YOU! I HAVE PROOF!*" He pointed the detective's notebook at the MonitOrb floating above the field and popped in the green cube. The screen suddenly presented to the entire stadium the footage of Alex blasting aliens. In stadium Jumbo-vision, Alex looked and sounded even more sinister.

Every head in the crowd turned and looked at Alex, who was standing on the field in his underpants. He swallowed a bite of Meteor-Dog and smiled weakly.

The entire stadium was suddenly hurled into
a state of panic. All through the stands, the
G'Daliens and the humans, suddenly confused
and terrified, ran in circles and leaped over seats
as they tried to get away from one another.

Mr. Illinois and LO-PEZ attempted to control the situation, but it was hopeless. GOR-DON watched the clamoring crowd from the field and grinned at an evil job well done. He was too pleased with himself to notice Herbert sneaking away from the SquadCar. Herbert ran over to Alex, Sammi, and Chicago.

"Hey, Herbalulu!" Chicago said.

"I'm glad you're here," Sammi said. "We've gotta get Alex out before this crowd kills him!"

"Or *not*," Herbert said, glaring at Alex.

"What's that supposed to mean?" Alex shot back, just as a giant Meteor-Cup full of green gooey juice hit him in the head. Herbert laughed. Alex pushed him.

"*Will you two stop it?!*" Sammi said, getting between them. She and Chicago quickly pulled the two of them into the Meteors' locker room.

Inside, Herbert immediately got right back in Alex's face. "You *ignoramus!* Are you happy now?! You've ruined everything, all because of your moronic video games!"

Alex squinted at Herbert menacingly. He slowly moved in even closer, until they were almost touching noses. "I'm going to ask you one more time. *What the heck is a video game?!*"

The raspy sound of a feeble voice made everyone turn around. *"Will you two ignorami knock it off?"*

A very old man floated out of a shadowy corner, hovering in a wheelchair with no wheels. He had a blanket over his lap and was bald and wrinkly. But there was something very familiar about him. "You two need to focus now," he wheezed. "You can settle your differences later if there is a later, which will depend upon whether or not you can focus now."

They all stared at him, confused. Alex turned to Herbert. "That sounds like something *you'd* say."

The old man sighed, "You're smarter than I remember, which isn't smart at all."

"Who are you?" Herbert asked.

"Perhaps this will jog your feeble memories," the old man said. He yanked the blanket away. Sitting on his lap was the AlienSlayer: 3-D! video game box.

Herbert shifted his anger from Alex to the old stranger. "*Thief!* You stole the game I stashed on the roof of Andretti's!" he said, then thought a second. "Wait. How did you know the combination?"

The old man laughed at him. "Please. Three, Fourteen, Eighteen, Seventy-nine? Einstein's birthday. It would've been obvious and predictable, even if I *wasn't* you."

They all froze.

"Wait, *what?*" Chicago asked no one in particular.

"Hey, you know what I just realized?" Alex pointed out to Herbert, "This old guy could *totally* be your grandfather."

Herbert and the old man looked at Alex. At the same time, they said, "Nice theory, Einstein."

"Hey! That's what he always says— Oh. Okay. He's you, but old. Got it." Alex said.

Herbert rushed to his older self. "So many questions. Let's start with the basics. Did we get into M.I.T.? Are we famous inventors? Do we still have a weird fear of damp cotton swabs?"

The old man looked at him.

"*Wow*, I was an annoying kid. No wonder I didn't have any friends until I got rich."

"You're rich?" Sammi said.

"You have friends?" Alex added.

"Wait, *what?*"
Chicago repeated.

Old Man Herbert led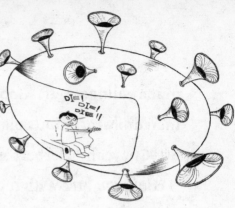
them out of the locker
room and into the dugout.
They looked up at the stands and onto the field.
Things had gotten much worse. Alex's violent,
alien-slaying memory played over and over
on the MonitOrb, and it was making everyone
act completely crazy. Humans and G'Daliens
were scrambling around, trying to escape one
another. Some were fighting. Others were trying
to get out, but GOR-DON had sealed the exits. He
was still in the middle of it all, laughing at the
chaos he'd caused, waiting for just the right time
to step up, lead the panicked sheep, and begin his
despotic rule.

"Whoa," Alex said. "So this is kinda *bad.*"

"Sure is." Old Man Herbert smiled over at his

much younger self. "Good thing we've got our incredibly ingenious plan to save the day."

"Oh, yeah," Herbert smiled back at him. "I couldn't agree with me more!" he said, and grabbed the box. "Okay. Listen up, everyone. First we're gonna need to locate the exact input frequency to that MonitOrb up there and override its projection receptors to match the holographic output of this game—" He stopped and wiggled the box to his ear like it was a

wrapped birthday present. He looked panicked as he tore open the AS:3-D! box. It was empty. He looked at the old man.

"What?" Old Man Herbert wheezed a laugh. "I hooked everything up weeks ago," he said. He hit a button on his AirChair, and the console to the AS:3-D! game flipped up in front of him. A satellite dish extended from behind and opened like a robotic umbrella. It pivoted and locked in on the MonitOrb hovering above the field. Then it beeped.

"The box was just for effect." He wheezed again. "I've been waiting a hundred years for you pea-brains to show up. Trust me, we're all set." He flipped a switch on the old AS:3-D! game. "Now let's do this. If I miss my afternoon nap, I get cranky."

CHAPTER 34

"Har har har!" GOR-DON's laugh was as loud as it was evil. "Showtime's over. Time to go to work, I suppose." He cleared his throat before he opened his horrid mouth to speak to the crowd. But what boomed out of the MonitOrb was not his voice.

"PEOPLE OF EARTH! WE INTERRUPT YOUR MINDLESS ENTERTAINMENT PROGRAMMING TO INFORM YOU THAT YOUR PLANET IS ABOUT TO BE INVADED—BY ALIENS!" Throughout the stands, the scrambling crowd stopped.

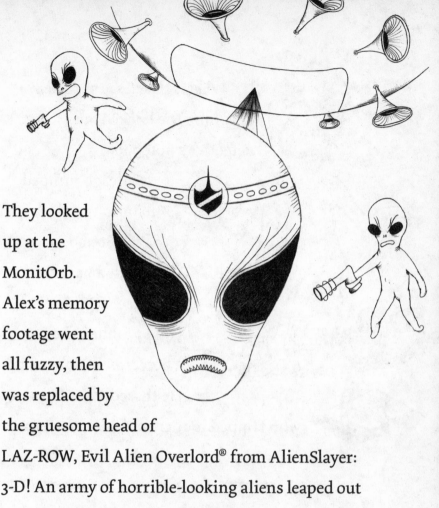

They looked up at the MonitOrb. Alex's memory footage went all fuzzy, then was replaced by the gruesome head of LAZ-ROW, Evil Alien Overlord® from AlienSlayer: 3-D! An army of horrible-looking aliens leaped out of the MonitOrb and hovered in midair in front of it. They were snarling, growling, and generally scaring the daylights out of every living thing in the stadium—even GOR-DON.

"*What is this?!*" he shrieked, dropping the tricked out detective's notebook.

Chicago jumped up onto the roof of the SquadCar. EL-ROY bounded past the stunned GOR-DON and grabbed the detective's notebook. He tossed it to Chicago,

who flipped it open and addressed the crowd.

"*MY FELLOW CITIZENS OF EARTH!*" Chicago's voice echoed. "*HUMANS AND G'DALIENS, LEND ME YOUR EARHOLES! WE ARE NOT ENEMIES!*" EL-ROY scrambled up onto the SquadCar, and Chicago put his arm around him. "*WE ARE ALL FRIENDS!*"

EL-ROY took the notebook. Even broadcast through the MonitOrb across the enormous stadium, his voice still sounded like that of a large chipmunk. *"HE'S RIGHT!"* chirped EL-ROY. *"WE MUST BAND TOGETHER TO DEFEAT THIS TRUE THREAT TO THE PLANET WE ALL LOVE AND SHARE!"*

Chicago glanced down at him. "Hey, that was *good*," he whispered. EL-ROY shrugged.

"YES!" Chicago's voice boomed to the rapt masses. *"WE MUST ASK HELP FROM THE ONLY ONES WHO CAN FIGHT THESE STRANGE AND HORRIBLE CREATURES—THE ALIEN SLAYERS!"*

The batwing doors opened under their feet.

Alex, Herbert, and Sammi stepped out. They wore the silver N.E.D. suits, and A.G. T-Ball–certified weighted boots. They were armed with the motion-sensor weapons from the AS:3-D! game. Alex gripped the TurboStaff, Herbert the BlasterShield, and Sammi wore the MegaMittens. They looked like superheroes—from the future. Above them, the evil LAZ-ROW and his fighters continued to hover, almost as if they were waiting for a challenger. Which they were.

THE ALIENSLAYERS

GOR-DON didn't know whether to be afraid or enraged. Either way, things were not going as planned.

"*Wait!*" he yelled. "This is some sort of trick! They're not *really* alien slayers! They can't be! I made all of that up!" On the sidelines, Mr. Illinois raised an eyebrow and shared a glance with GOR-DON. He pulled out his spare detective's notebook, this one a more basic model, and scribbled down a quick "to-do" list for himself:

1. *Get chubby, annoying janitor's confession.*
2. *Write up case report.*
3. *Pick up flowers for Mrs. Illinois.*

"No! No! This isn't how it's supposed to work!" GOR-DON squealed, but he was quickly drowned out by Chicago, who addressed the crowd one last time. *"EVERYONE, PLEASE! TAKE YOUR SEATS, BUCKLE IN, AND LET'S ALL OF US CHEER ON THESE BRAVE WARRIORS!"* As the fans strapped back in to their seats, Chicago gave the thumbs-up to Old Man Herbert, who hovered in his AirChair on the sidelines, beside the giant antigravity switch.

He flipped the gravity off.

The Meteor-Dome jolted and hummed. The bases flew up into the air again. The buckled-in fans hovered in their seats. And GOR-DON, too befuddled to strap himself down in time, went hurling straight up, screaming as he slammed into the bottom of the MonitOrb. His blobby flesh flattened against its smooth metallic underbelly like pancake batter on a bowling ball.

S P L A T !!!

GOR-DON had a front row seat as Alex, Herbert, and Sammi leaped up onto the three floating bases and faced the alien-projecting MonitOrb. The crowd began to cheer them on.

"You guys ready for this?" Sammi yelled.

Herbert smirked at her. "I think we can handle it."

"*Let's blow these slime-sucking freaks into a gazillion space-chunks!*" Alex suddenly blurted out.

The other two shared a look, and Alex wondered for a split second where he'd heard that before. Down on the field, Old Man Herbert pressed *PLAY* on the AS: 3-D! console.

The 3-D holographic creatures attacked. Herbert fumbled with his BlasterShield, but recovered just in time to deflect a massive laser blast. *KAPOWWWZZT!!*

"*Whoa!*" he hollered.

"Impressively lifelike graphics!" He turned to the others. "Guys! Behind me and let's move in!" He leaped into the air, blocking shots meant for his partners, and burst out laughing. "I've never felt so alive!" he shouted as he jumped from base to base, deflecting blasts intended for his teammates.

Sammi moved in. She thrust her MegaMitten-enhanced fists of fury into the torsos of the holographic attackers. She leaped and ninja-flipped as she delivered blow after deadly blow. But for every alien she killed, two more new ones leaped out of the MonitOrb screen.

"There are too many of them!" she yelled.

HI-YA!!!

"I've got to pull back!"

"Take cover!" Alex yelled, leaping from second to third base to avoid being blasted by a hologram. "I've got this!" He spun his TurboStaff like a baton, whipping up a laser whirlpool. It blasted through a gang of attackers, laying them to holographic waste. As a few 3-D adversaries broke through his firepower, he stopped spinning and wielded the deadly staff like a Kung Fu master. He clubbed and speared the snarling, pixilated beasts until they were a mere trickle coming out of the MonitOrb.

With the death of each vicious holograph, the aliens let out an ear-piercing squeal before exploding. And each time, it was answered by the even louder roar of the crowd.

"We're winning! Great job, you guys!" yelled Herbert.

"So are we done?" Sammi asked, kind of bored.

"No," Alex said as he squinted at the screen. "That was just the appetizer. Now comes the main course." He wondered to himself how he could possibly know this.

Sure enough, LAZ-ROW, Evil Alien Overlord®, rose from out of the MonitOrb. The gigantic, terrifying creature shot lasers out of its eyes, and its tail whipped around a large, electro-zapping spike.

It looked down at the three puny humans and blurted out an evil *laugh*.

"Let's waste this lizard!" Sammi said, straight-faced.

The three of them leaped into the air and landed together, on one another's shoulders. Alex stood on the base, Herbert on his shoulders, and Sammi on the top. They began to sway, shifting their weight back and forth. The base-on-a-chain swung like an upside-down pendulum, each time getting closer and closer to the video-villain.

LAZ-ROW puffed his horrible self up and prepared to laser-fry the three silver heroes. His

tail drew up behind him. All at once, he fired his laser eyes and lunged his tail. Herbert, Sammi, and Alex launched themselves into the air in three different directions. Herbert blocked the laser shot.

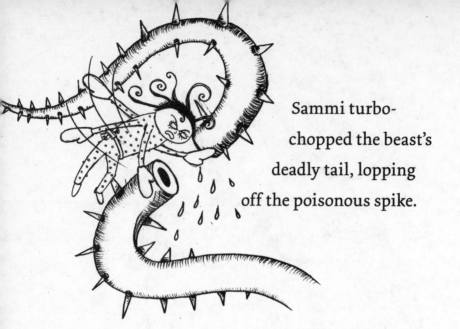

Sammi turbo-
chopped the beast's
deadly tail, lopping
off the poisonous spike.

Alex thrust his TurboStaff into
its laser-blasting eye. The alien leader tossed its
head back and let out a thunderous shriek.

Its awful voice shook the stadium and its walls, echoing across the city of Merwinsville. Its red flesh exploded into a million holographic chunks, and it disappeared in a puff of very realistic-looking video-vapor.

The screen went black.

The crowd went wild.

Alex, Herbert, and Sammi stood together on a base and drifted down as they soaked up the cheers pulsing from the stands, from humans and G'Daliens alike. The three heroes smiled at one another as they touched down onto the field.

"That was awesome!" Alex said.

"Yeah," Herbert agreed. "I never thought I'd say this about a video game, but that was actually kind of fun."

Alex looked at him. "A video what?"

Old Man Herbert flipped off the antigravity switch. As the fans flooded the field, an explosion of confetti blasted into the air, raining down and covering the field like a blanket of brightly colored snow. Humans and G'Daliens in the crowd lifted up Alex, Herbert, and Sammi and carried them out of the Meteor-Dome, into the streets.

The return of gravity left GOR-DON in a tough spot—hanging by a tentacle from the bottom of the MonitOrb. He clung as long as he could, then *POP!* He finally dropped to the field like a sack of slugs.

An orange vest hit him in the head.

Mr. Illinois stepped up and loomed over him with a dustpan and broom. "I'll get your confession for my case report Monday morning. First, I assume you haven't forgotten how to use these," he said. "I need this field clean for my son's practice tomorrow, so I want all this confetti swept up by dawn, *Gorgonzola*." He smiled at the rumpled pile of alien and walked out of the stadium to join the celebration.

IT'S GOR-DON.

CHAPTER 35

The crowd carried Alex, Herbert, and Sammi through the streets of Merwinsville, across the plaza, and to the steps of the museum, where they were presented with a ridiculously large, gold-plated keycard to the city. The three of them waved and smiled as they took the poster-sized keycard. Herbert scanned the crowd.

"Do you guys see Old Man Me anywhere?"

Alex shook his head. "I hope I made it to a hundred and ten," he said as he waved to the crowd below.

"I doubt I make it to *eleven*," Sammi said. "I blew off, like, a half-dozen prepaid, nonrefundable activities today—my parents are gonna *kill* me." Alex looked at her and she smiled back at him. "Totally worth it, though."

The three of them waved and smiled as they slowly walked backward, up the stairs. They reached the giant museum door. Herbert reached behind him and tried to turn the handle. "The door's locked!" he whispered. Alex offered his brand-new, giant gold keycard to the city. Herbert scoffed. "That doesn't actually open any doors, you ignora—"

Alex swiped it through a slot on the giant door handle, and it clicked open. "Nice theory, *Slewg*," he said.

The three of them slipped inside. The confused crowd watched them disappear. They all glanced at one another, then rushed up the steps after the three of them.

Chicago was standing inside

the museum door. "I thought you guys might need help with your exit strategy again," he said.

As the crowd reached the door and started banging on it, Alex stepped forward. "Chicago, we've got something to tell you. We're, uh, not from here."

Chicago chuckled at them. "I know. You're from the past, came through a wormhole, *blah, blah, blah.*"

They stared at him. "Old Man You told me all about it. You should get to know that guy. He's like you, but older. And much, *much* cooler."

"Yeah, thanks for the advice." Herbert said. The WHUMPING on the door suddenly grew louder, and the door began to creak open from the force of the mob.

"Go before your fans tear you apart. I'll slow 'em down." They looked at him, and he smiled. "I still can't believe I thought this town was boring! Come back soon, okay?"

Sammi blurted out, "We will!" She grabbed the giant gold keycard to the city and handed it to him. Then she, Alex, and Herbert ran across the lobby, toward the Hall of Human History.

The crowd burst in, and Chicago turned to face them. He looked down the opposite direction, to the far end of the museum. "Hey! There they go!" he yelled. The mob ran off in

the wrong direction. Chicago smiled, put on his
Meteors cap, and walked out the museum door.

CHAPTER 36

Alex, Herbert, and Sammi stood before the fake cave in the prehistoric diorama. "I was thinking maybe we should invite Chicago to our time someday," Sammi said. "I bet he'd like it."

"Hmm," Alex said, pretending to actually consider it. "I don't think that's a good idea. Besides, there are only three suits, one for each of us—*Just us.*"

"Actually," Herbert said, "I have one more that came with the video game. I could easily modify it for Chicago."

Alex shot Herbert a look of death. He stepped up to him like he was going to hit him. "For the last time—*what the heck is a video game?*"

Herbert glanced at Sammi and asked, "Alex—what do you think we fought in that stadium back there?"

Alex grinned. "What, did *you* lose your memory, too? The three of us just saved our city—and probably our *planet*—by kicking some seriously *gnarly* alien butt! We're heroes! We're *alien slayers!*"

Herbert chuckled. "Okay, listen. I hate to inform you of this, but that whole thing was just a vid—" Sammi suddenly flipped the switch

on Alex's belt. The blue, shimmering wormhole opened up and began sucking Alex toward it. He yelled, *"Last one home's a rotten alien larvae pod!"* and dived in.

Herbert looked at Sammi. She shrugged. "So he thinks he just saved the world. That's a pretty cool memory. I say we let him keep it." She flipped her own switch and dived into the wormhole.

Herbert fired up his own suit and looked back at the woolly mammoth. He smiled, then turned and stepped toward the warm, blue shimmering light. He felt it pulling him in. He closed his eyes and leaned toward the rock.

In a flash, both Herbert and his wormhole were gone.

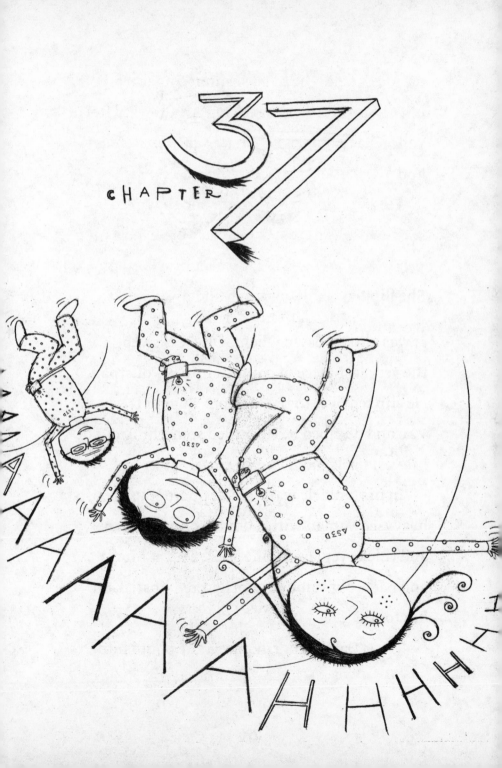

It was almost dawn when GOR-DON swept
the very last piece of confetti into his dustpan.
He slinked over to the Meteors' dugout trash
can and dumped it. He pulled something out of
his vest pocket and looked closely at it.

In his tentacle was a small photograph of a
heavyset woman with a double chin, a hairnet,
and thick eyeglasses. She smiled up at him,
and had a big smudge of bright red lipstick on
her tooth.

The G'Dalien angrily threw the photo into

To Gordon,
Love,
Marion.
We'll
always
have meatloaf
mondays

the trash can. His lip quivered a bit, and he
quickly reached back in to retrieve it. But
something else caught his eye. He reached
down with his tentacle and pulled it out. The
box was old and faded, but the words were still

legible: *ALIENSLAYER: 3-D! VIDEO GAME SYSTEM.*
Scowling up at him from the box was LAZ-ROW,
Evil Alien Overlord®. The bitter G'Dalien's
face twitched.

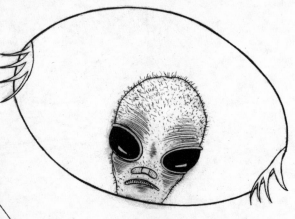

He tucked the box under
his vest and skulked out of
the stadium. Sneaking through
the shadows, he oozed home just ahead of the
pink morning haze of another perfect day in
Merwinsville.

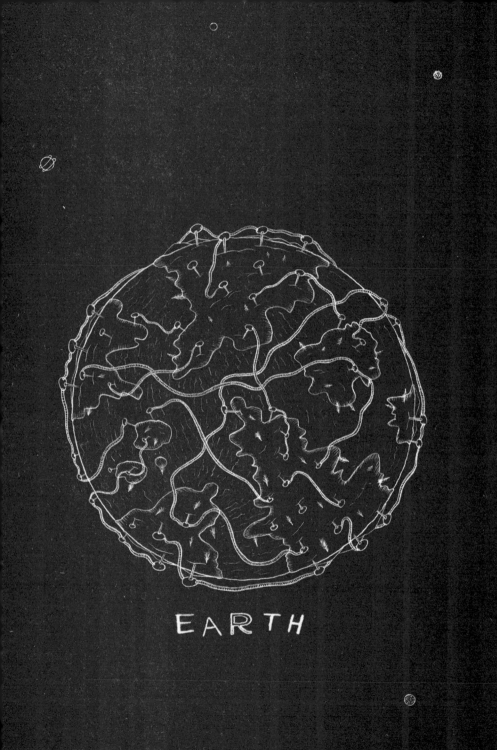

EARTH

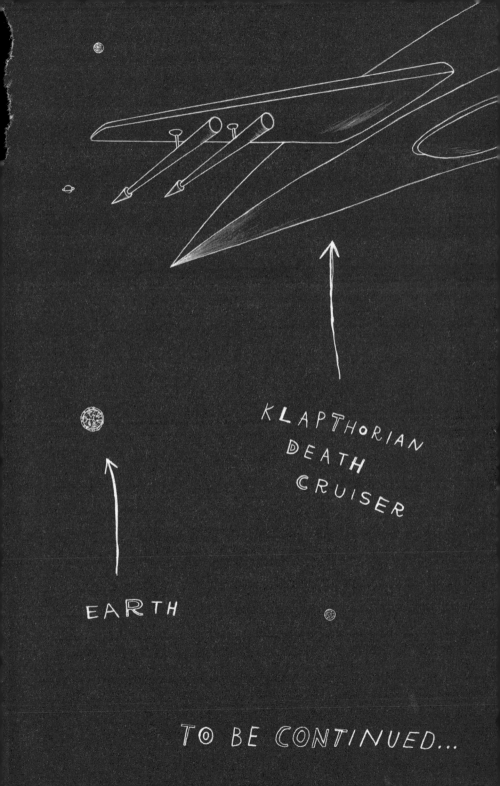